SUMMER AT THE LAKEHOUSE CAFE

SOPHIE HAYDON

BAY BOOKS

Summer at the Lakehouse Café
by Sophie Haydon

A staunchly independent solo mum. A winemaker who has lost his family. A summer in which to learn to trust again.

—The Mackenzies—
A Place Called Home
Secrets at Parata Bay
Escape to Shelter Springs
What you See in the Stars
Second Chance at Whisper Creek
Summer at the Lakehouse Café

—Lantern Bay—
Yours to Give
Yours to Treasure
Yours to Cherish
Yours to Keep
Yours Forever
Yours to Love

For more information about this author, visit:
https://sophiehaydon.com

ISBN 978-199-102110-6 (Amazon Print)
ISBN 978-199-102129-8 (Draft2Digital Print)
© 2017 Diana Fraser

CONTENTS

CHAPTER ONE

The sun hadn't yet risen above the mountains when Lizzi Burnett drove down the dusty track to the secluded bay. She parked at the very end of the track, where the lake—a pale blue in the early-morning light—was framed between stands of tall pine trees.

She lowered the window of her car and cut the engine. Lulled by the sound of lapping water and the honeyed fragrance of wild lupins and dried grass, she sighed and closed her eyes.

She loved these rare moments when she was alone with nothing but the pristine ring of mountains that cradled the Mackenzie basin, with the township of Shelter Springs and Shelter Lake at its center. High up in New Zealand's South Island, the world felt fresh, beautiful and full of hope again, reminding her of how she'd felt when she was young, growing up by the sea. It seemed a long time ago.

She opened the car door, noting the rust which would have to last another year before she could afford to do anything about it, and closed it quietly, reluctant to disturb the birdsong.

Slinging her bag over her shoulder, she walked to the grassy bank above the small beach. She was wearing her swimming togs under her clothes and was about to undress when she paused and sat on the springy grass instead.

Maybe it was because she was tired, but she felt different this morning. She glanced across to the other side of the lake to her cottage beside The Lakehouse Café where she and her daughter lived. But Aimee wasn't there this morning. She was staying at her grandfather's house in Akaroa for the week. It meant Lizzi could devote her entire attention to the café. It also meant that she felt a yawning gap in her heart and life which she hadn't anticipated.

Life was so busy that she thought she'd enjoy a few days on her own, focusing on what she needed to get done. And she had, but not without missing Aimee every second of every day.

She wondered how on earth she'd get on when Aimee was old enough to leave home. But even though that was years away—Aimee was only six—she knew. Once you had a child, they never left you, you never stopped worrying about them.

The sun peeped over the mountain and spread its rich light over the lake and the grassy plains, turning them to fire. The vision was so majestic, so ridiculous, Lizzi laughed and, instead of stripping and running into the water, she lay on the grass. The last wisps of clouds were already evaporating under what would be another scorching hot day.

She was so lucky. Aimee was safe. She was safe. And she loved her work, running the café. She plucked a piece of grass, popped it into her mouth and began chewing it as her mind wandered over what she had to do that day.

Suddenly she frowned. The soothing sound of the gentle waves breaking over the pebbles was overtaken by a rhythmic splash. She narrowed her eyes as she tried to place the cause. Not a bird—it was too rhythmic, and not the wind —it was too powerful. A wave of nausea washed over her and she sat up. She hated surprises, hated the unpredictable.

She didn't see him to begin with. Then the light from the sun flashed on the white plume of water as an arm struck into the ice blue of the lake's surface. The angle of the sun made it difficult to see clearly. It was followed by another and then another, as the swimmer came ever closer to the bay. She looked around in panic. It was *her* bay. She never saw anyone else here. She grabbed her bag, pulled on her cardigan and walked quickly toward the car, hoping to get there before the lone swimmer reached the beach.

She hurried across the few hundred yards which separated the grassy bank from her car, and opened the car door. She hesitated then. This was ridiculous. Why should her adrenaline surge at the thought of a stranger? Why should she dive straight away into a fight or flight response when she came across something she hadn't predicted? She knew why. But she was sick of it. Sick of running, sick of being scared. It was these thoughts which made her turn to the swimmer. But it was what she saw next which made her stand stock-still.

A man rose up from the lake, the bright light of the sun nearly blinding her as it reflected off the water which ran in thick rivulets from his body. He waded toward her, thrusting forward with an energy and power which had her completely fixated. His leg muscles were long and taut, pushing the water out of his way, creating waves that rippled out across the lake as if he were a one-man tsunami.

He was wearing shorts which clung to his thighs and his hips, revealing every contour. She lifted her eyes to his stomach—which showed the kind of six-pack only seen on models—and to his chest and shoulders which had the breadth and strength of a swimmer. He swept his hair from his face and twisted around, looking up toward the mountains, whose white caps flamed like torches in the morning sun.

Lizzi licked her lips and drew in a deep breath. Who was this man with the looks of a god, or at least of Daniel Craig, and what was he doing out here, in the middle of nowhere—*her* nowhere to be precise?

He turned suddenly and saw her. She felt her cheeks flame as ruddy as the mountain tops as she realized how she appeared—standing, openly eyeing him up. A grin spread across his face, revealing even white teeth and dimples in his cheeks. Seemed he didn't mind being eyed up.

He waved one tanned, strong arm. "Morning!"

"Morning!" she said, too huskily. She cleared her throat. "Good morning!" This time it sounded too loud in the stillness of the bay.

He continued toward her, his feet apparently unaware of the stones on which he was walking. She focused fixedly on his eyes. *Damn!* They were of a blue to compete with the sky. But she daren't look anywhere else for fear she'd focus on that physique and not raise her eyes again.

"It's a beauty," he said.

"Certainly is." She couldn't disagree with that.

"Do you think it'll last?"

What? Her face must have conveyed her confusion because he laughed and the sheer happiness she heard there brought a smile to her own lips.

"They've forecast rain later," he explained.

"Oh," she said as she suddenly realized what they were talking about. "They're always forecasting rain to make the farmers more optimistic. But it usually doesn't. Rain, I mean. Or," she added as an afterthought as she tried to get her brain into gear, "make the farmers optimistic."

Another heart-stopping grin. She had to ask.

"Where did you come from?" They were miles from Shelter Springs, and there were no other cars around. If he'd answered that he'd dropped from the sky in a parachute or emerged from the water itself, like some kind of lake spirit—the kind women dreamed of at night—she didn't think she'd be surprised.

"I ran here."

"Oh!" Turned out a rational explanation was more surprising.

He narrowed his eyes against the increasing brightness of the sun and indicated the motel a couple of miles away, low against the horizon, on the edge of Shelter Springs township. "I'm staying over at the motel with my mates. Thought I'd fit in an early morning run. And"—he glanced at the lake—"when I saw this inlet, I had to go for a swim. What an amazing place." He turned to her suddenly. "Are you about to go for a swim?"

She flexed her hand on the door handle, as her mind raced over how to answer. "Yes. Well, I was. But, I don't know. Probably not now."

"It's pretty cold, but good when you get in."

She smiled. "After the first gasp you look up to the mountains, and you forget to be cold."

He followed her gaze. "Takes you out of yourself. Makes you forget your problems."

She stared at him. She couldn't believe that someone that gorgeous could have any problems. Stupid thing to think. Good looks didn't stop the world from dumping on you.

"So do you come here often?" He grinned and rolled his eyes. "The oldest chat-up line in the book."

She narrowed her eyes and looked away. Was he flirting with her? She couldn't remember the last time anyone had tried that. Maybe a few clichéd lines in the café, but nothing for real. She decided the best thing to do was ignore it.

"Yes, I like to come here when I can." She nearly said when Aimee wasn't with her. But that would be revealing too much. She'd learned over the years that you didn't do that. That way lay trouble. "It's close to town, but you feel like you're away from it all. How about you? Visiting?"

"I'm here for a week, catching up with friends and hoping to do some business. I'm in the winery industry and looking around for new investments."

"Well, there are a few wineries west of here which might interest you."

"Yes, I'm looking at one today."

"Which one?"

"Tussock Hills."

"Ah, yes, I heard they were interested in selling up. Pretty remote though."

He shrugged. "Remote doesn't bother me. I live on Waiheke Island. My family has been there for generations."

"Waiheke? I've never been there, but I hear it's beautiful. Warm climate, beautiful place. And yet you want to move?"

"There's more to a place than weather and scenery. There's only me now. I've been looking for a new place to start things over. And this place appeals." He glanced at her. "In a number of ways."

She nodded. She, of all people, understood the urge to begin again. But she didn't have the luxury of picking up her life, her child, and her job, and moving on. She had no money for one thing. And, for another, this was Aimee's home.

"It looks like some of the land's already been sold for development." He gestured toward a long, low house that had been recently built on the lake front.

"Oh that. I'm hoping no one will buy it. I've never seen anyone there and it's too far from Queenstown and Wanaka to be of interest to many."

The man grunted as he took in the scene. "It's got a great view."

"It's even better from the house."

He glanced at her. "Is it?"

"Yeah. It's built on a rise, and you can see across the lake, over toward the town and beyond."

He grunted and ran up to the side of the house. "You're right. You can even see Lonely Peak from here."

"And Kairua Peak."

"Kairua Peak? Which one's that? Come and show me."

Lizzi relaxed her grip on the door handle and pushed the door closed. Despite her wariness, she couldn't resist the invitation; couldn't resist the man, it would seem. She walked up to him, her only thoughts were of his tanned body, strong and masculine. She imagined how those muscles would feel under her fingertips, flexing in response to her touch. She looked away quickly and pointed to the mountain.

"It's the peak directly behind that long ridge."

"Oh, yes."

But when she glanced at him, it was her he was looking at. He smiled again, and she felt something melt inside. Those warm blue eyes, that smile... So engaging, so good-humored and, so seductive... She looked away quickly. She should leave. Now.

When she looked back, he'd sat on the grass, his arms behind, supporting him, as he surveyed the view. She knew she should leave. This man was trouble. She knew what she had to do, but, instead, she sat a little distance from him and folded her legs beneath her. She plucked a long piece of grass and twisted it around her finger, refusing to listen to that warning voice in her head.

"If I had the money I'd buy this like a shot," she said.

"A bit isolated. That wouldn't worry you?"

"I like being on my own. But—" She stopped suddenly.

"But?"

She shrugged. "It doesn't matter."

He frowned. "Aren't you hot with that cardigan on?"

She plucked at the sleeve. It was ridiculous, but she'd got into the habit of covering up, after years of her ex-husband demanding it. She shrugged. "No. I'm fine." But even as she said the words, the heat of the sun—or was it simply his proximity—caused a flush to her cheeks.

"Really?" he said wryly. "I'd hate to see what you wore in winter."

"More of the same." She looked at him and grinned. "Three layers deep. And some."

He grunted a laugh. "Shame."

"Why?"

"It's always a shame to cover up something—or someone —beautiful."

"Oh." She turned away.

"Sorry," he said, looking anywhere but at her. "I didn't mean to be personal, to make you feel uncomfortable. It's just a fact."

Was it? It had been years since she'd felt beautiful, since she'd believed anyone who'd told her that. Years in which she'd ignored her physical self. She rose and folded her arms. "I'd best be off."

He also stood. "What time is it?"

Without thinking she pulled up her sleeve to check her watch. "Nearly seven-thirty." She caught his gaze, looking at her forearm, white from the lack of sun.

"You really do like to cover up, don't you?" He smiled, but there was a curiosity in his eyes. "Is that why you come to a remote spot to swim?"

For a few moments, she couldn't take her eyes off his— his blue eyes seemed more violet now, warmer, full of interest.

She tried to shake her head, but there was something in his gaze which stopped her, something which demanded the truth. Or at least a semblance of it. "Habit. It's silly really." She gnawed her lip and then made a decision. Let him see. She was sick of hiding. Still holding his gaze, she pushed up both sleeves and held them out. "I've a few burns I'm self-conscious of."

Her cheeks flushed as she focused on her arms, not wanting to see his reaction. The burns weren't extensive, but what they did was make people ask questions, questions she didn't want to answer.

"How did they happen?"

She still focused on her arms. "Accidents. Accidents happen sometimes."

He nodded and then, to her surprise, he reached out and gently, so gently, it was like the touch of a feather against her skin, he swept up her arm, moving over the shiny scar tissue, gently over the ridges of puckered skin. She felt an echo of the sensation—sometimes acute, sometimes numbed by the nerve damage—deep inside her body, in places which had no right to respond to his touch.

His eyes followed the movement of his finger, which hovered briefly over her wrist, before pulling away. "Accidents *do* happen. But not like that."

She looked at him sharply. How on earth did he know? Not that she was prepared to ask. Not that she was prepared to continue the conversation. She wanted it out in the open and it was. Trouble was, his response had been more unsettling than hiding her scars from him.

"I'm in the hospitality industry. Accidents happen there," she said, deliberately vague.

"Sure." He shook his head again, contradicting his response.

Her phone went and she took it from her bag and shaded the glare with her hand to see the message. She smiled at Aimee's message. "It's my daughter. She wants me to call her." When she saw the reaction on his face, part of her wished she hadn't spoken.

"You have a daughter? How old is she?"

"Six."

"You're lucky. Must be great."

"It... has its moments."

"Anyway, you call her. I need to get back." He extended his hand. She took it and tried to suppress the charge of lust which shot through her at the warmth and pressure of his hand around hers. "It was great meeting you." He moved away too soon and pulled on his running shoes.

"And you." She smiled briefly, trying to adjust to this sudden withdrawal of interest. "Enjoy the rest of your stay. When—" She managed to stop herself from asking when he'd be leaving.

"Sorry?" He turned.

She shook her head. "Nothing. Anyhow, I'd best be off."

He shrugged on his t-shirt. His shorts had dried off a little but still clung teasingly to his shape.

"I don't know your name," she called out as he picked up pace.

He turned and ran backward for a few paces. "I guess not!" He grinned and continued on his way.

She'd taken a risk, showing her scars. She'd thought from his response that he hadn't been sickened by what he'd seen. But it seemed she was wrong. Seemed he couldn't get away from her fast enough and that he had no interest in knowing her name or any intention of seeing her again.

She looked away from the sight of him running along the track to the highway, and strode to the water's edge, pulling her cardigan and dress off as she went. She tossed them to one side, kicked her shoes off and ran into the water and dived, her body brushing the stony bed before emerging into the sunlight. Her body was numb from the sudden blast of cool water. If only she could numb her heart with equal ease.

Pete ran along the path, unable to wipe a grin from his face. He'd recognized her straight away from the photo her brother had shown him. But the photo had nothing on the real woman. When he'd first seen her, he'd thought he'd drowned and gone to heaven. That chestnut hair that fell in waves around her face, that bright smile, those brown eyes that melted and caressed you. They had the same effect as chocolate—irresistible and, he feared, addictive.

And then her scars. If she was trying to put him off, she'd failed. His experience in the army had shown him many things: self-inflicted harm, harm inflicted by others, and accidental harm. And her scars were definitely not accidental. They'd done nothing more than intrigue him, and move him. Somehow their contrast to her beauty had simply made her appear more beautiful.

And then there was the expression on her face as he'd left. No, he hadn't done the predictable thing and asked her out, even though he could see she was expecting it. He hadn't asked to see her again because there was no need. He'd be seeing her in a few hours, even if she didn't know it.

CHAPTER TWO

The brass doorbell jangled, and Lizzi looked up from the counter as the door swung open and Gemma Mackenzie entered the café.

She grinned at the redhead who'd quickly become her best friend since Gemma had first arrived in New Zealand several years earlier.

"Coffee?" asked Lizzi as she wiped her hands on a towel and moved toward the espresso machine. She didn't have to wait for an answer. Gemma always wanted a coffee.

"Sure," sighed Gemma. "I'm exhausted. Why didn't you tell me having kids was so exhausting?"

Lizzi banged the coffee basket on the counter, pressed the coffee firmly in, and twisted it into the machine. "Because if anyone told the truth, there wouldn't be any more children. Besides, not much use telling you when you were already pregnant."

Gemma pulled a face. "Very funny."

Lizzi grinned as she switched on the noisy steamer. She deftly added the steamed milk to the coffee, putting her trademark swirl on top, and slid the mug along the counter. "So what is it you've been doing that's so exhausting?"

"Dallas and Cassandra are visiting. So we've their kids and Morgan's and Rebecca's, because I somehow found myself suggesting the parents leave the kids with Callum and me for the weekend, giving them some alone time."

Lizzi laughed. "I bet Callum would have preferred it to be the other way around."

"He says so, but you should see him with the kids. He has a blast doing all the things he never allows himself time for. He took the older kids off horse trekking, leaving me getting messy in the sandpit with the littlies." She took a sip of coffee. "Strange how boys go straight for the diggers and end up crashing them together while Daniella and Violet Rose made a nice seating arrangements for their Barbies."

"They'll learn."

"Yeah. But hopefully not the hard way."

"Is there any other way?"

Gemma and Lizzi exchanged knowing glances. They both knew all about hard. Gemma's life had been anything but simple, even after she'd married Callum, but now their marriage was as strong as the mountains which surrounded Glencoe, the Mackenzie's South Island estate. But Gemma wasn't dwelling on her past as she took another sip of coffee and turned her perceptive gaze to Lizzi. "Still no progress with the café?"

Lizzi wiped the bench. This was an issue on which Gemma and Lizzi *didn't* see eye to eye. "No," she said quickly.

"Care to elaborate?"

"No."

"If you need investors in the café, you know Callum and I will jump at the chance."

"And why would you jump at investing in a small café?"

"Because we have implicit faith in the owner?" ventured Gemma.

"And because you're too generous. You know as well as I do that it's not a good investment if it's split too many ways. No, there's only one way forward, and that's for me to own it outright."

"*If* Charles pulls out. He hasn't yet, has he?"

Lizzi grimaced. She'd been trying to forget her ex-husband's threat to sell the café from under her. There was some naïve part of her which hoped that if she ignored the threat, it wouldn't happen. "No. He probably won't. He's always saying stuff like that just to rile me."

"I don't get him." Gemma glanced at the photograph of Lizzi, Charles and Aimee on the wall—Charles, tall and broad wearing his full army uniform. "He's Aimee's father, a war hero, and his family home is in the Mackenzie Country. Why would he sell the café?"

"He's a bully, he's never forgiven me for leaving him, and he no longer has to appear supportive now his mother has died."

Gemma grunted with annoyance. "But he has a new wife, a new life in Indonesia."

"Doesn't stop him from wanting to inflict hurt."

"Why?"

"Because he can. Because that's what makes him tick." Lizzi dried up the few remaining glasses and stacked them on the shelf. "Anyway, I'd best get the function room finished. Max has hired it for the evening. He and some of his mates spent the week in Queenstown and stopped off here for a few days on their way to Christchurch." Lizzi indicated the function room. "He's in there now, Skyping some real estate agent about yet more property in Queenstown."

"I don't know why you don't tell him about the café."

"Because I'm a big girl and want to stand on my own two feet."

Gemma rose from her stool and stood on tiptoe to get a look. She whistled softly under her breath. "Your brother just gets better and better."

"Like cheese?"

"No way! Only a sister could say that. More like a rich, smoky pinot noir. More intoxicating, more depth..." Gemma flashed her eyes in mock flirtation.

Lizzi shook her head and grinned as the bell jangled again. Lizzi looked over. "Don't let your husband hear you saying that."

"Saying what?" Callum Mackenzie dropped a kiss on the blushing Gemma.

"Saying how much she likes red wine when you're starting to grow white," said Lizzi with a grin.

Gemma shot her a grateful look.

Callum put his arm around Gemma and pulled her to him and kissed her on the lips. Gemma moaned lightly as Callum's kiss grew from a peck to something far more sensuous.

Lizzi balled up a wet tea towel and threw it at them. "Go get a room." It didn't have any effect. "Or twenty, in the case of Glencoe."

She sighed. She loved them both, but the sight of so much lust was hard to take when her own love life was about as lush as a desert.

"See you guys." She left them to it, grabbed the tray of glasses, and walked into the function room.

Max looked up from his laptop. "Hey, sis!"

"Hey, you." She began setting the table. "Bought up all of Queenstown yet?"

"Not yet. Just finessing the finances on some property. We should sign next month." He looked over her shoulder and narrowed his eyes. "Is that Gemma?" He made an appreciative noise in his throat. "Pity she's taken."

"Ha! Even if she wasn't, there's no way you'd last more than six months—a year tops. You're a confirmed bachelor."

"You have such a low opinion of me."

"Might be low, but it's accurate."

"Maybe I haven't met the right woman yet."

"What's this? My big brother thinking of settling down?"

He looked at her as if she'd gone mad. "No way. I just meant if I meet the right woman, I might..." He shrugged. "Hell, you're right. I love women too much to settle for one."

"What is it with you and commitment?"

She plumped up the cushions on the settees which faced the windows overlooking the lake and picked up a half-drunk beer bottle. Max's. She turned to him and wondered, not for the first time, why he was so different to the rest of their siblings. At the first sign of neediness, he was off.

He closed his laptop and jumped up and gave her a peck on the cheek, plucking his beer from her hand as he did so. "We don't go together. Me and commitment, we're at opposite ends of the spectrum. Polar opposites. Chalk and cheese. Yin and yang."

"Ha! Those two fit together."

"Scratch that, then. But you get my drift." He grabbed some nuts from the bowl and tossed them into his mouth, munching as he looked at her with a frown. "I hear your ex-mother-in-law passed away."

Lizzi looked away. "Yeah."

"You okay?"

"Sure. I'll miss her though. Margaret was a wonderful woman."

"Totally different to her son, then."

"Totally. She was full of love—"

"And he wasn't," said Max, bitterly, shaking his head. "If I'd have known what I know now, he wouldn't have been able to walk away so easily."

She reached out and placed her hand on his, trying to calm him. "Hey! It's over. Done with."

But he didn't look comforted. Instead, he held her gaze. "I wish it was, Lizzi. But you haven't been able to move on yet. I'd love to see you happy again."

She laughed, surprised. "That's strange. Margaret said something like that just before she died." Lizzi frowned, trying to remember. Then she shrugged. "Something about everyone needing love—that life's better like that. I can't remember the exact words."

"She was a wise woman." He sighed and looked around at the table which she'd already laid out with snacks, ready for him and his friends. "So, are you joining us?"

"No. I've work to do." She gestured toward her small cottage which lay adjacent to the café. "I'm off home. Katie's going to serve dinner. It's all prepared. I'll come along later."

"Make sure you do, Lizzi. I won't be seeing so much of you after this deal goes through. I'll be staying put in Queenstown for a while."

"There are a lot worse places to be stuck." The bell went in the café. "I'll see you later then." She turned around to find herself staring at the man she'd met by the lake—the man with no name, the man whose body she couldn't stop thinking about. The memory of those thoughts made her flush with embarrassment.

"Pete!" said Max. "Good, you came early; it gives me a chance to introduce my gorgeous sister. Lizzi, this is Pete Marshall. Pete, Lizzi Burnett." He looked from one to the other, expectantly, his gaze lingering on Lizzi. "Lizzi! You're blushing. I can't remember you ever blushing before."

She shot him a filthy look.

Pete grinned and stuck out a hand toward her. "We've met already. Although I had fewer clothes on then, of course."

"What?" spluttered Max from behind her.

The blushing deepened if anything, but she found herself shaking his hand anyway. And the strong, enveloping touch of his hand did nothing to straighten her thoughts. She pulled away. "Pete! That's your name, I mean."

He laughed. "Yes."

Max shook his head in confusion. "So how did you two meet?"

"Uh, Pete will tell you. I've... got to go." She gestured toward her house. "Work to do." She smiled briefly and walked around Pete, trying desperately to ignore the fact that he was even hotter in clothes. She was tall, but he was taller. He made her feel so... so damn feminine.

She didn't look back as she walked into the kitchen and gathered her things.

"So how did you meet Lizzi?" she heard Max ask.

Lizzi kept her head down, fiddling with some paperwork under the counter, wanting to hear Pete's reply, but not wanting them to know she was listening.

There was a small pause, and then Pete spoke. "She drew me to shore like a siren."

Her blush deepened as the word echoed around her mind. *Siren.* Siren? It had been *him* who'd looked godlike, wading to shore, with his amazing underwear model physique. Emerging from the lake as if the water were his element, as if he were someone from another world.

Had she had an equally memorable effect on him?

She dropped the paperwork and stood, and they both grinned at her.

She held up a batch of invoices. "Forgot something." And, without looking back she went next door to her cottage. It didn't matter if it was a memorable meeting or not, she told herself sternly. She'd done with relationships. Her marriage had been a disaster, leaving her a single mum, the manager of a café she part-owned with her ex-husband, and wary of any man who looked at her twice.

No, she thought as she opened her laptop at the café's spreadsheet, this was real, this was her future—hers and Aimee's. And she wasn't about to do anything rash which would jeopardize it.

It was past ten by the time Max and his friends had finished for the night. She could hear them calling out their thanks to Katie and the odd mention of Lizzi's name. No doubt Max was wondering where she was. Knowing him, he'd drop by her cottage before he went to the motel where he was staying with his mates.

She didn't have to make an appearance at the café—she could rely on Katie to close up. She'd been working with Lizzi since Gemma had left the café several years before.

Lizzi went to the sideboard and drew out a whiskey bottle and two glasses. She was stepping outside onto the deck to place them on the table when there was a knock at the door.

"You don't have to knock!" she called out. "Just come on in."

She smiled to herself as she continued outside. Since when had Max ever respected her privacy? She heard his footsteps cross the polished boards of her cottage, heard them hesitate on the threshold. She sighed with pleasure at the view. "Out here! Come and join me. It's a wonderful night. Those stars." Still, there was no sound, no retort. "I have whiskey!" she tempted. But the silence continued, and she swung around suddenly to find it wasn't her brother standing there, but Pete. He stood on the porch, a bottle in his hand, and that sexy smile on his face.

He shook his head. "Sorry to startle you. Max suggested I come on over. He had some conference call with the UK to make at the motel."

Lizzi cleared her throat. "Of course he does. He never stops working."

"And nor do you, by the looks of things." He indicated the papers around the laptop.

"Making the most of the fact my daughter's staying with my family in Akaroa."

He nodded slowly. "It must be difficult, juggling work with family."

"Yep." She folded her arms across her chest, determined not to let his sympathy get to her. She fidgeted, glanced at him and then away again, uncertain. What the hell? She was never uncertain.

"Whiskey? Another thing you can do while your daughter's not around."

"Drink whiskey with a stranger?"

"But I'm not a stranger. We've already met. Your brother's even introduced us. So..." He held up the bottle. "Drink? Max will kill me if I don't manage to get you to have at least one drink with me. A 'thank you' for the wonderful meal. That's all."

She smiled uncertainly, unable to prevent herself from being softened by his words. "Okay. That would be nice. Thanks." She turned to the view. "Max loves this view so I thought we'd drink here. Is that all right with you?"

"More than all right." He placed the bottle on the sun-bleached wooden table and walked toward the edge of the deck. She watched him as he looked out at the dark lake which lapped onto the reed beds close by. The inside lamp caught the brightness of his white shirt and glanced off his cheekbones and jawline. He was *so* good-looking. What on earth was he doing here, with her?

She took a deep breath of the night air, which smelled of damp earth and sweet grasses blowing in from the hills, and poured them both a drink. He took it from her, his fingers briefly touching hers.

"*Salut,*" he said quietly.

"*Salut.*" She clinked her glass against his. "To Max's continued success with the resort."

"To his success." He inclined his head closer to hers. "Although I doubt he needs our best wishes—success seems to follow him around."

"He's always been like that. Whatever he's tried his hand at, he's made a success of. Except for relationships, that is."

Pete frowned. "And why's that, do you think?" He took a sip of his whiskey.

Lizzi shrugged. "Comes too easily, I think. He's never had to fight for anything, or anyone."

"Or maybe, he's simply never met the right woman." His intimate gaze made her heart race.

"Funny. He said the same thing." She stepped away, needing to distance herself. She picked up a plate of antipasto which she'd put together for her supper, and offered it to him.

"No thanks. Your dinner was superb."

She took something and chewed it, immediately wishing she hadn't.

"Hungry?"

She shook her head and swallowed. "No. Just can't stop myself from offering people food." She shrugged. "It's what I do best."

"It's an excellent thing to do best." He smiled, and she couldn't help wondering what he did best. If his sensual smile was anything to go by, it didn't take a genius to work out.

"So..." She needed to change the subject. "How do you know Max?"

"We met in Auckland, years ago. He went out with my sister for a short while, before she—" He stopped abruptly and took a swig of whiskey.

"Before she?" Lizzi prompted.

"Before she went overseas. Anyway, we hit it off, so we stayed in touch." He looked around at the hills, now silver under the starlight. "It was Max who suggested I look at wineries around here." His wandering gaze rested on Lizzi again. "I'm glad he did. What I see interests me, very much."

She swallowed. "So do you think you'll buy Tussock Hills?"

He smiled, apparently recognizing her need to keep the conversation focused on business. "Probably. It's ripe for investment. I can see where I can add value."

"So you're really interested?" She leaned against the table.

"Yes. If and when I can sell Whisper Creek, I'll be here like a shot. It's just the sort of challenge I want—fresh and far away from my old life. Sometimes, Lizzi, you just want to move on. Leave your old life behind and start again. Do you ever feel like that?"

She huffed. "All the time. But"—she swirled the amber liquid around the glass—"you can begin again even if you stay in the same place. At least I hope so."

"I guess you're tied to the café."

"Yes. And, I've Aimee to consider, and she's happy here. We have a lot of friends who are like family. And then there's my family—they're not far away—you must have heard about them."

"Ah, yes. Belendroit, in Lantern Bay, the Connelly homestead. I visited Max there once a few years ago. It's the stuff of story books."

She nodded, remembering Belendroit. "It is. Growing up there, running wild around the garden, the house, the beach and bay, was"—she looked up at him—"perfect."

"And you have no need to return to perfection? Despite the lanterns your mum strung everywhere to guide you lot home?" He smiled. "Max told me about them."

"No. There's no going back in this world. That's one thing I've learned." Silence fell on them and she suddenly realized how quickly their conversation had moved beyond the superficial. "Would you like another whiskey?"

"Sure, thanks." He walked over to her and held out his

glass. She topped it up. "I'm sorry I ran off like that this morning."

"How did you know who I was?"

"Max showed me a photo."

"Ah, and you knew we'd be meeting up later."

"Yes." He rolled back on his heels, his eyes never leaving hers, alight with flirtation. "I knew."

"You were teasing me."

"I guess."

"So... the only question is, why?"

"You looked so... contained, standing there on the shore, I wanted to rattle you a little. *Were* you rattled?"

"No, of course not. Nothing rattles me."

"And if it did, you certainly wouldn't admit it."

"Exactly."

"Fair enough."

"So tell me about the winery." She sat on the swing seat, and he moved beside her. Too close now. It had been fine to think of her big brother sitting there, and leaning her head against his shoulder as they looked out upon the black lake. But now, she shifted away slightly and folded her arms.

She listened as he talked about the winery—the land, the current owners, the grapes—and absorbed not only what he was saying, but how he was saying it—deciphering his personality behind his words. She didn't trust her intense attraction to him. She'd been suckered in once before by trusting her instinct. She'd been wrong then. She wouldn't let it happen again.

"Isn't this purchase a little... impulsive? I mean, you hardly know anything about the area."

He pushed off the floor lightly, making the chair rock back and forward. She relaxed under its swaying rhythm and took a sip of whiskey.

"I'm a creature of impulse," he said with a grin. "I know all I need to know. It's beautiful, peaceful, close to the ski fields, has a lake to swim in. Not to mention a café which serves great food. What else is there to know?"

"Everything," she said, with a seriousness which made his smile fade. "You can't trust your impulses."

"I can."

"I can't."

He shrugged. "Two impulsive creatures aren't a good recipe, anyway. And you know all about recipes."

"Oh yes. It's all about timing."

He narrowed his eyes. "In what way?"

He nudged the swing seat again, and the rocking made her slide closer to him. She should move. She took another sip of whiskey instead.

"Add the eggs too soon to a cake mix, and it curdles. Add the stock all at once to a risotto, and it goes gluggy. You have to take it slowly, little by little, checking it out, judging it every minute of the way, making sure everything's on track. Timing is everything."

She paused, wondering if he understood, wondering if she was mad for saying it, when all the while her senses ran riot. Her fingers itched to run along his tanned and muscled forearm which cradled his glass. She could feel the heat of his thigh against hers. And there was nothing slow about the melting inside her. She feared there'd be nothing left of her soon except a whimpering mess of a woman who'd actually *do* what she imagined—slide onto his lap, lift his chin and kiss those sensual lips.

He nodded and rose, making the seat swing abruptly and Lizzi acutely aware of his absence.

"So," he said, observing her from the other side of the

deck. "My usual 'jump in and test the water' approach won't be effective here."

"Uh-uh." She shook her head. But she rose too, drawn by his irresistible crooked smile.

"Then I shall thank you for the dinner, the whiskey and your company and…"

"And?" She really shouldn't have moved so close to him. It was like he had some spell around him, some magnetic energy, which drew her to him, making her forget her best intentions, and, instead, focus on a faint waft of aftershave which lingered in the air. He swayed closer to her, or did she sway closer to him?

"And ask you out." Her heart missed a beat. "What are you doing during the week?" he continued.

"Working."

"Weekend?"

"Working. And Aimee's home."

"Then I'll pay court while you're working."

She spluttered a laugh. "Pay court?"

"Indeed. That's what us slow and steady Aucklanders do when we like someone."

"You like me?"

"Of course. Is that so hard to understand? You're beautiful and charming. What's not to like?"

"Shall I give you a list?"

"No, I prefer to find out for myself. So, the café tomorrow?"

"That would be nice."

She waited with bated breath, wondering if he'd kiss her. Instead, he swayed away from her and smiled that smile —that spoke of fun and laughter and teasing seduction—and stepped toward the door. "Until tomorrow, then."

"Tomorrow."

Lizzi couldn't stop grinning as she locked the door behind her and stepped out onto the deck and watched his shadow walk off down the street, toward the motel. Then the old clock chimed one, and she realized how late it was. She had to be up early to open the café. She went inside and was brushing her teeth when her phone rang out a cha-cha rhythm which indicated a text from Max. Smiling as she continued to brush—she really shouldn't let Aimee choose the ringtone on her phone, they were so wildly inappropriate—she walked into the lounge and picked up her phone.

What do you think of Pete? Max must have heard Pete return to the motel.

He's nice, she replied.

Carrot cake is nice. Lemonade is nice, he replied.

Okay. Handsome, charming, funny... all the things I don't trust.

There was a pause before Max's reply came through. She could see he was typing, but he must have deleted his message and retyped.

He's a good guy. Don't be scared. Not all men are like Charles. He's thousands of miles away. He can't hurt you now.

Tears pricked Lizzi's eyes. After her big brother had discovered the abuse Lizzi had received at Charles's hands, he'd been incandescent with rage. Lizzi had never seen Max in such a state before. She'd been relieved that Charles had disappeared overseas because Charles was ex-army, six foot six with muscles to match, and she'd been scared Max would have come off worse. But knowing how much Max cared for her warmed her soul.

Sure. Night, big bro.

Night.

Lizzi tossed the phone onto the sofa and went to the bathroom to rinse her mouth out. She looked up and saw herself in the mirror. Her eyes had lost the brightness which Pete's presence had brought. Instead, there was the shadow of distrust firmly back in place. Just the mention of Charles's name made it come flooding back.

She walked over to the window. Holding on to the sides of the frames, she took one last breath of the sweet night air and closed the window. She picked up one of Aimee's toys and tossed it into the toy basket.

Max was wrong. Charles might be thousands of miles away, but he could still hurt her. He could take away her and Aimee's livelihood, and he could keep her scared by his constant threats of visiting. Oh yes, Max was quite wrong. Charles still controlled her as effectively as if they were both still living together.

CHAPTER THREE

"Hey there!" One of the café's regulars called to Pete as he entered the café.

"Hi Tony!"

"You again? You've been in every day for the last three weeks!" Tony beckoned, and Pete walked over to him. "Reckon you've your eye on something more than Lizzi's good cooking." He winked at Pete.

Pete glanced at Lizzi who, luckily, was out of earshot. "Yeah," he said as Aimee spotted him as she came in from school. "Can't deny it. Eh, Aimee?"

"What?" asked Aimee with a puzzled frown.

"We've a regular thing going with your homework."

Aimee sighed at the reminder and emptied her school bag on the table and stood, dejected, arms at her side, pouting. "Math."

Pete picked up her math textbook and flicked through it. "Changed a bit since my day but I was always pretty sharp at math. Want to give it a shot now?"

"How about some food first," said Lizzi, placing two hot drinks and a plate of sandwiches and cakes onto a low table in a corner, around which were placed leather settees which had seen better days. Shelves, filled with junk shop finds of old books and curios, lined the walls above them.

"Looks great," said Pete, watching Lizzi as she sorted Aimee out, taking away the remains of her packed lunch, and her PE bag. There was something amazingly sexy about a woman caring for her child. She was so unaware, so self-less, as she made sure Aimee was settled. Her auburn hair was caught in a French twist, which revealed her sun-kissed nose and sweeping cheekbones.

It was only when she stood back and caught his gaze that she flushed, and Pete thought there was something even sexier about a woman who was suddenly aware she was being undressed by a man's eyes. The awareness was in her tawny eyes which flashed with a desire which reflected his own.

Slow, Pete reminded himself, slow.

"Um," she said. "So... how was your day? Any news on Whisper Creek?"

"Yep. I met up with James Mackenzie at Glencoe this afternoon. I'm flying up to Waiheke Island tomorrow to prepare things for him. He's interested in buying me out."

"That's fantastic! I thought he might be. That's why I passed on your brochure and DVD to Gemma."

He grinned. "I wondered how he'd got hold of them. Well, thank you, Lizzi. I'll have to repay you with dinner. Tonight?"

Lizzi glanced at Aimee who was playing on her phone, happy not to have adult attention on her. "How about I cook *you* dinner?"

"You've done that every evening for the past couple of weeks!"

"Are you complaining?"

"You know I'm not," said Pete. "I've appreciated every minute of it. Your company, the food, the wine, and afterward, the—"

She cleared her throat, and frowned, nodding her head toward Aimee.

"The coffee, was all I was going to say. You make great coffee."

She frowned harder. "Right," she said, obviously not believing him.

She was correct. He'd nearly let it slip that the moment he looked forward to was when he kissed her, directly before he left. They'd begun with a kiss on each cheek before moving onto an exquisitely gentle kiss on the lips. He'd forced himself to remain at that level for as long as he could. But then, the previous evening, he'd felt a change in Lizzi. It had been *her* hand which had snaked around his neck, her fingers which splayed and shifted up into his hair, gripping it tight as she opened her mouth under his. The kiss had deepened and the memory of Lizzi's responsiveness under his mouth, his hands, and the feel of her pressed tightly against his aroused body, had him itching to take her in his arms again.

"See you!" Tony called as he left the café.

Lizzi jumped as if caught out. "Have a good evening!" She went and bolted the door.

Pete walked over to the café's deck, which shared the same view as Lizzi's cottage next door. He was aware of Lizzi joining him. "I'm going to miss that view when I'm away."

"How long do you think you'll be gone?"

"No longer than a week. A quick trip to Whisper Creek, and a catch-up with some friends."

"Then you'll be back."

"Dead right. I've a winery to buy. And... I have other news."

"What's that?"

He pulled a real estate leaflet from his pocket. "It's not only the winery I'm going to buy. Turns out the house by the lake is owned by the same people who own the winery." He handed her the leaflet and waited for her reaction. She loved the place as much as he did and they'd driven out to the spot where they'd met a few times over the past few weeks. He'd fallen harder each time they'd gone.

She frowned and took the leaflet from him and looked at it as if she couldn't believe it. "Te Mararua? The stone house by the lake?"

"That's the one. The owners furnished it but now the wife says it's too remote so they want to sell the whole lot— fully furnished." He paused, unable to contain a grin.

"Oh."

It was his turn to frown. He'd expected pleasure, excitement even, but not the single grunt she gave. She handed the leaflet to him.

"You're not happy for me?"

"Um, yes, of course. It's just..."

"Just what?"

"Unexpected."

"But you knew I was looking for a place, and you knew I loved that place."

"But you didn't think to tell me about it?"

"I thought it'd be a surprise. I can see it is, but not the right sort. What's up?"

"Nothing. Oh, I'm being stupid." She sighed. "I've always loved that place. Somehow I imagined it could be mine."

"Play your cards right, and—"

He stopped, arrested by her suddenly blank expression. She turned away abruptly and walked around the other side of the café's bench top. Cursing to himself, he went over to Aimee.

"Break's over. Math time, kiddo."

But as Aimee went through her math, he found it increasingly hard to concentrate. What on earth had made him say that? Apart from the fact he should have known it would frighten Lizzi away—she'd made it clear as daylight she wanted to progress things slowly—what had he been about to say? *Play your cards right, and it could be yours?* Why would he say that when he didn't mean it?

He'd come to the South Island looking for a new beginning, not to settle down with anyone. Since Ellen had died, he'd only had short-term relationships—he'd made sure of that. It had been easy at first as no one compared to his first love, and even easier when he joined the army. And then afterward? He'd mixed with a party crowd in Auckland for whom nothing was ever serious. And now here he was teaching math to a six-year-old kid and practically proposing to her mother!

He'd agreed to take it slowly with Lizzi but somewhere along the way, on one of those evenings out on the cottage's veranda, as the territorial cries of the black stilt—the kaki—cut through the silence, and the cool, fresh smell of the high country had drenched the air, when the kisses had grown hotter, things had sped up for him. He hadn't even noticed, let alone admitted it to himself. Now that he had, he felt uneasy. And, one look at Lizzi's stern expression, he could see she wasn't so sure either.

He shifted his focus to Aimee whose half-hearted attempts at the math problem had him shaking his head.

"Come on, Aimee. You know better than that! Give it another go."

"But I'm tired!"

"When do you have to have it finished by?"

"Tomorrow. Miss Clark said I'd get a detention if I didn't."

"Then, tired or not, you'd better finish it."

He looked up and saw Lizzi's stern expression had intensified. She stood there, frozen, until their gaze met and she moved away. He narrowed his eyes. For some reason she looked shocked, her complexion paler than usual.

He took a sip of coffee, irritated with himself. He'd probably spoken too unsympathetically to Aimee. She wasn't his daughter. But he hadn't spent every day with Aimee and Lizzi without discovering the root of Aimee's problem with school—her charm. She managed to wriggle out of anything she didn't like because she could. And he knew it wouldn't help her in the long run. He knew that because his sister had been the same.

Lizzi finished up in the kitchen, all the while watching Pete and Aimee. The past few weeks had been amazing. She'd felt the knot of her emotions unfurl like a reluctant spring flower under the influence of Pete's slow wooing. But now she'd opened up she felt vulnerable and, looking at Pete and Aimee interact, she suddenly felt like it was still winter and the chill hurt her to the core.

First the fact that he was about to buy the house she'd looked longingly out onto for years, in what she considered to be *her* bay. Second, he was about to buy a winery close by. She felt she'd got onto a narrow moving walkway which led only one way—and she wasn't sure it was the way she wanted to go.

And now, seeing him move beyond encouragement with Aimee's homework. She'd been taken straight to one of the many scenes between Charles and Aimee, where Charles had lost patience with Aimee, insisting on discipline, insisting on her doing as she was told, completely forgetting that she was a young child. Seeing Pete talk firmly to her, sent a chill down her spine. It was nothing like Charles, and yet... could it be a warning of things to come?

"Aimee?" she called. "Why not leave your homework for now? Your favorite program's on the TV."

Aimee didn't need asking twice and scooted off to the cottage.

"What's up, Lizzi?" For once Pete was frowning.

"What makes you think anything's up?"

"Maybe because you couldn't hide your feelings if you tried?"

She grunted. "You seem to have got to know me pretty well in only a few short weeks."

"I've made a study of it. Of you."

Her heart thudded. Again, that intensity, that focus—Charles had been the same. She fidgeted with the cling film she was stretching over a salad they'd have for dinner later. "Okay, whatever. It's just Aimee."

"What about Aimee?"

"Pete, you've been great with her these past weeks. Her teachers have all said how much more confident she is in class, especially with her math. But I wish you weren't so... so tough with her over it."

"You think I'm tough? You should have seen my old man with me!"

"I know that's how many people get taught, but Aimee's sensitive."

"She's fine. She didn't bat an eyelid when I told her to re-do those sums. I wasn't tough, believe me. She has to get used to the real world."

Lizzi gasped and looked away. She opened her mouth to speak, but she felt as if she'd been winded, couldn't seem to find any air.

"Lizzi?" Pete's fingers curled around her arm, and an icy blast of fear slid right through her like a knife. "Lizzi, what is it? Are you okay?"

She shook her head and turned to him. No, she wasn't okay. Not when she heard her abusive ex-husband's words on Pete's tongue. Charles had always justified his excessive disciplinarian style by saying that she had to get used to the real world. It was like the toll of a bell, clanging loud and clear in her head.

"I'm fine. It's a bit hot in here. I'm going outside for some air."

She walked quickly toward the lake, not caring whether Pete followed or stayed put. She took a deep breath, willing the fresh chill air that now swept down from the snowy tops of the mountains to wipe away her fears. Then she looked across the lake to the house of her dreams—the house that looked across toward hers.

His footfall rang hollow on the boardwalk as he approached her. He stopped short. She suddenly felt trapped.

"Hey, Lizzi. If you don't want me to help Aimee, then that's fine. I thought I was doing you both a favor."

She turned around. He had the sun behind him so that she couldn't see his features clearly—just his outline, tall, athletic, holding himself incredibly upright and she suddenly got it. And at the same time, she felt that slice of fear again, except this time, it didn't disappear.

"You were in the army, weren't you?"

"Yes, that's right. Didn't I tell you?"

"No, you didn't." She licked her dry lips and swallowed, her hands finding a handful of her shirt and bunching it into her fists, as she tried to control the adrenaline that pumped through her body, making her want to run, to get the hell out. He stood there, suddenly unknown and unknowable— representing everything she didn't want.

"What of it? There's probably a heap of other things I haven't told you. Do you want to know my favorite color? Star sign, you probably already know."

"I don't want to know more, Pete. I'm sorry, but I think it's best if you go."

She could hardly see the frown and confusion in his silhouette against the harsh afternoon sun, but she could sense it. "I'm sorry," she repeated and tried to walk past him, back up to the café. He put out his hand and took hers. She jerked to a stop, and the fear surged, and she cried out and pulled her hand from his and ran toward the café.

It wasn't until Lizzi entered the café and looked out that she saw Pete hadn't moved. He stood, hands thrust into his trousers, looking out across the lake.

How could she have missed that military bearing? That honed body which only military discipline could develop? Okay, she might have been ultrasensitive about his making Aimee start the sum at the beginning again, but it felt like the thin end of the wedge. A warning which she'd ignored to her peril last time.

She followed his gaze out toward the stone house, which would soon be his. These last weeks, she'd been so entranced by him, by his flirtation and attentions she hadn't noticed he'd started to take over her life, weaving his own around her until she felt she was stuck, immobile, trapped at the center of a sticky cocoon, like prey.

Then he walked around the outside of the café and disappeared.

Heart thumping, mouth dry with fear, Lizzi tried to figure out why the panic had been swiftly replaced by a hollow, empty feeling.

What had she done? She thrust her fingers through her hair and twisted around in anguish. Had she narrowly averted disaster? Or, had she rejected the best thing that had happened to her in years?

CHAPTER FOUR

I t had been four weeks since Pete had walked away from the café, and returned to Auckland. Four weeks and she hadn't received a text or a phone call. Not that she could blame him. Why would he? She'd made it quite clear that she didn't want to pursue the relationship. But still, every time the doorbell went, every time her phone rang, she hoped it would be him.

Lizzi sighed. She was one confused woman. And that was due to Charles. And, it was also due to Charles that Lizzi was now making the half-hour return journey to Shelter Springs after her meeting with the bank manager. Charles had given her an ultimatum—buy me out, or the café's going on the market.

At least it stopped her thinking about Pete. Instead, she was going over and over in her mind the conversation she'd had with her bank manager. Would he give her the loan? He'd seemed impressed at first with all the facts and figures she'd given him. But he'd been less impressed at her refusal to include any members of her family in her plans.

Yes, she understood that her father's wealth would

mean the loan would be a rubber-stamp job. But no way in this world was she accepting anyone's help in re-financing The Lakehouse Café. *Her* café. Apart from the fact that her father had made it quite clear what he thought about her going into the hospitality business, she was doing this alone, or not at all. If the worst came to the worst, she and Aimee would simply move to a different town and begin again. But it *had* to be on her terms. She *had* to be independent. She, alone, had to be in control of their lives. No one else. She refused to go there again.

She plucked at her shirt that was sticking to her back. Goodness, it was hot! She checked the temperature—ninety-five degrees. At least it would mean the café would be busy. She hoped Katie was coping okay without her.

With the air conditioning long since dead, she opened the window and let in the warm breeze and grassy scent of the Mackenzie Country. When she first saw the lake below her, she sighed with relief. She was home again.

She pulled up outside the café. There were people everywhere, tourists stopping off between Queenstown and the east coast, checking out the lake activities, the picturesque church and, at night, the stars. The population of the Mackenzie Basin swelled in the summer months which was when the café brought in most of its annual revenue. It was good money, but not enough to satisfy the bank, it would seem.

She grabbed her laptop, stepped out the car, and paused to admire the café. It was everything to her. She'd poured the last three years of her life into it and had transformed it into the place it was today—the coolest café between Queenstown and Christchurch. It was situated in a prime location in Shelter Springs, poised slightly above the lake with a wide frontage, decked all the way along to make the most of the expansive views of the lake and the high, snowy mountains beyond. She couldn't bear the thought of losing it.

She entered the café and went straight into the back office. Katie popped her head around the door. "Iced coffee?"

"Wonderful, thanks! How have things been here?"

"Busy. But manageable. I'll go and get you that coffee. You look beat."

Before Lizzi could switch on her laptop, a car drew up outside and Lizzi saw Aimee jump out, followed quickly by Gemma's daughter and niece and nephew, with Gemma not far behind. The door burst open, and Aimee launched herself at Lizzi. Lizzi bent and gave her a big hug and kiss. "And how's my girl, then?"

"You've been ages," Aimee said, her six-year-old cupid mouth pouting for all it was worth.

"You've had fun with Gemma and Violet Rose, and her niece and nephew, Lily and Joe, haven't you?"

"Yes. Except they kept wanting to swim in their pool."

"And you didn't."

"I don't like swimming."

Lizzi sighed. Aimee was nervous of most physical sports and refused to participate, no matter how much Lizzi encouraged her.

"Aimee! Come and play!" Lily Mackenzie called from the cottage garden.

"Go on, love. I'll make you all some afternoon tea in a while. I'll call you then."

Lizzi watched Aimee disappear with a sigh. "Has she been okay?" she asked Gemma.

"She's been fine, honest," said Gemma. "She's just going through a nervous phase." Katie slid iced coffees in front of

Lizzi and Gemma, and returned to the café. "Any luck at the bank?"

Lizzi pulled the coffee toward her and took a sip, relishing the chill air of the clinking ice cubes which wafted up to her flushed cheeks. "They said they'd give me their final decision at the end of today, after they've had a chance to go over my spreadsheets. But it's not looking good. I simply don't have the turnover to cover the costs." Lizzi glanced at Katie and the other waitresses. "Even if they went for it I'd have to let at least one waitress go, and I'd have to work all hours to meet the repayments."

Gemma reached over and took Lizzi's hands in hers, her eyes full of sympathy. "Why won't you accept our offer?"

"Because I can't be dependent on anyone anymore. Charles's father bought the business for me as settlement for the divorce and wanted to give me the money for the improvements." Lizzi bit her lip.

"But you wouldn't let him. You insisted it should be a loan." Gemma sighed. "And now he's dead and Charles has inherited the loan and has called it in." Gemma shook her head. "I just don't understand why Charles would do this to you."

Lizzi rose to her feet. "Because he can. He wants to cash up all his New Zealand assets and channel the money into his estate in Indonesia. Aimee's inheritance is secure and untouchable, as is right, thanks to Charles's father. No thanks to Charles, of course," she added bitterly.

"Can't you talk to him? Make him see what position that's leaving you and Aimee in?"

Lizzi shook her head. Gemma only had the barest idea what her ex-husband was like, and it had to stay that way. "No. I tried, but he's made a new life for himself there, and that's all he's interested in."

"So you won't accept another partner?"

"No, I won't. I never want to put myself in this position again. I either own The Lakehouse Café outright, or I don't own it at all."

Lizzi took another sip of her coffee, holding it firmly in her hands as she looked around the café which had become a focus for locals, not just visitors. With a reputation for imaginative and wholesome food, a quirky retro interior, art-filled walls, and expansive lakeside decks, it had something for everyone.

"I can't bear to see you leave the café," said Gemma. "Look what you've made it. Callum said it was like an old-school transport café before you took it over."

Lizzi followed Gemma's gaze and felt heartsick all over again. Every piece of decoration, every cushion, every little object picked up for a song from second-hand shops around New Zealand, had been selected according to strict criteria. One, Lizzi loved it, two Lizzi loved it. And three... well, that she loved it. They were narrow criteria, but it had ended up working strangely well. Not least because she'd been strict with herself and halved the number of things she wanted to bring into the café. The other half found its way into her own home. The result was a bright, welcoming series of rooms which felt more like a home than a café.

She swallowed hard as a lump rose in her throat at the thought of losing this place that was so much more to her than a business. "It'll be fine," she said.

"Say it again like you mean it," said Gemma, sitting in her chair and watching Lizzi like a hawk.

Lizzi grunted. "You know I can't."

"Well, our offer stays on the table. If you want it, call me. Okay?"

"You're so good to me."

"You're my friend. Besides, you were good to me when I first came to New Zealand. Giving me my first job."

Lizzi grinned. "Because Callum told me to."

"Yeah, well, I didn't know that at the time. But you were still very good to me. And I'll never forget it. So promise me you won't forget our offer?"

Lizzi trailed her finger through the condensation on the outside of her glass. She hadn't allowed herself to think beyond the bank loan. But if the bank didn't come through? Then she owed it to Aimee to accept Gemma's loan. But she'd cross that bridge when she came to it. "I..."

Gemma reached forward and took Lizzi's hands in hers. "Look, I'm being selfish here. I need somewhere to hang my paintings."

"Yeah, right. With the way your career is going, you won't have any shortage of venues, in New Zealand or overseas."

"But none of them will mean as much to me as this place." Gemma stood. "Anyway, we can talk about it again later, after you've heard from the bank. I'd best be off. Callum will be wondering where I am."

Lizzi rose and walked with Gemma to the door, exchanging a few words with a departing customer as she did so. In the entrance way, Gemma stopped by a wall of photographs which showed the history of the building, the land and its original owners—Lizzi's ex-husband's family, the Burnetts. Gemma pointed to one at the center of the group. It was of Lizzi, and Aimee as a baby, with Charles. Beside it was another of Charles in full military gear being awarded a medal for bravery after his last tour in Iraq. "There aren't many divorcees who have photos of their ex-husband on full show."

Lizzi shifted the frame, so it was sitting straight on the

wall. "There aren't many who have exes who are local war heroes. Besides, it's there for Aimee."

"Pity he didn't show the same loyalty as you when it came to selling out his half of the business."

Lizzi shrugged. She'd come to look at the photo as if it were of a stranger, distancing herself from the man who had been her husband. "He wants to improve his grandparents' estate in Indonesia. He wants to settle there." And she wanted the same thing—he couldn't be far enough away from her and Aimee, as far as she was concerned.

"And he doesn't seem to much care what happens to you or to Aimee in the process."

"No. He's a hard man. We're his past, and he wants rid of it."

Gemma shook her head. "His loss. Hey"—she gave Lizzi a hug—"make sure you let me know what the bank manager says. Okay?"

"Yes, sure."

Gemma walked down the path, called the kids over, and then stopped suddenly. "Oh, I meant to say, James rang today. He's bought Pete's winery. Looks like James is going to stay up in Waiheke for a while." She raised an eyebrow. "So you know what that means?"

Lizzi knew exactly what that meant, but she wasn't in the mood to discuss the wreck that was her love life. "That no woman on Waiheke will be safe from his charms for the duration of James's visit?"

"Well, yes, there is that. But you know what I mean. I hear Pete's returning to Shelter Springs."

Lizzi's heart beat a little faster. "Really?" she said, trying to sound only vaguely interested.

"Yes, really. And you can't fool me, Lizzi Burnett. He's hot, and he's hot for you."

"I doubt it. Not after how we parted."

Gemma groaned and shook her head. "Give yourself a break, girl. Text him and ask him out. I dare you!" She continued to the car, waving behind her. "See you later!"

Lizzi watched as she drove off, wishing for once she could be Gemma with everything sorted—a loving husband, beautiful kids and a secure life in Glencoe—the wealthiest estate in the district.

But she wasn't. She might not blame herself for the collapse of her marriage, or her deep-seated need to be the sole owner of the café, but she sure blamed herself for turning Pete away.

Max had given her an earful, of course. He'd insisted she and Pete would be good together. And he'd told her to stop being so damned scared. But it wasn't that easy.

Max didn't know what it was like to live with a man whose mood changed swiftly and unpredictably. He didn't know what it was like to keep quiet while you were being hit, not wanting your daughter to walk in and see what was happening; what it was like while you watched a cigarette being lit, knowing it would shortly be stubbed out, but not in the ashtray.

No, those close to her might know some of what happened, but there was no way they could completely understand, not without having experienced what she'd gone through. No one knew but her. And no one but her could understand her need never to be trapped in a relationship—business or personal—which could make her vulnerable.

Pete would make some woman a wonderful husband, but it wouldn't be her. Friends, maybe, she thought as she tidied up the café. But only if she explained what had happened—not everything, but enough for him to understand.

Yes, friends would be good. But lovers? No. She shook her head as her mind wandered at the thought, teasing her with visions of his body, of memories of the effect of his lips on hers. *Damn!* She rolled up the cloth and threw it into the sink. *Damn!*

"Better have some milk as well, please," said Pete to the shopkeeper.

"Here for a while, then?" the shopkeeper asked.

"You could say that. I've bought the house at the other end of the lake. The two-story stone property."

"Welcome to Shelter Springs. It's a very cool house. Look forward to seeing you around. And if there's anything special you'd like bringing in, let me know."

"Will do." Pete picked up the bags and walked out of the shop and straight into Lizzi, her auburn hair softly framing her face, her honeyed eyes betraying nerves. It took all his control not to reach out and pull her to him and kiss her senseless. He cleared his throat. She wouldn't be here for him.

"Lizzi!" He held open the shop door for her. "You going in?"

She shook her head. "No."

He frowned, noting that she wasn't holding anything, that she obviously wasn't shopping. She simply stood, arms at her sides, motionless. "Oh." There was a long pause. "It's good to see you."

"And you," she said eagerly. "I mean. That's why I'm here. I wanted to see you."

His eyes widened in surprise. "You wanted to see me?"

She had the grace to look embarrassed. "I know. After what I said. Look, I'm sorry, Pete. I wanted a chance to explain why I said what I said." She shook her head. "It's hard to explain. But—"

"It's okay. I get it. You don't want a relationship with me. It's simple. You don't have to explain anything to me."

"I do. Because it's *not* simple. If we're going to be virtually neighbors, we can't avoid each other. I need to explain, to clear the air." She looked around with an anguished expression and Pete would have felt sorry for her if he hadn't been so frustrated. "We can't talk here. Do you want to come by the cottage later?"

He was silent for a moment. Lizzi's abrupt about-face four weeks before had left him confounded. Part of him felt hurt and confused at her sudden rejection, but there was also a part of him which was relieved. He'd found himself on the slippery path of commitment without even knowing it. And to be given an escape route had been something of a relief. At least to start with. But as the days had passed he'd found he couldn't stop thinking about her, whether he liked it or not.

"For Aimee's sake, at least," she added. "It would be good to be friends. To clear the air."

"For Aimee, sure," he said quickly. At least on *that*, they could both agree. "What time?"

"Eight? I'll have supper for you. You can say hi to Aimee before she goes to bed."

"Sounds good. I'll see you at eight."

"Sure," she stepped away. "Eight. That's cool."

He forced a smile. "See you later, then." He walked on the sidewalk to his car, trying to think of anything but the brightness of her rich brown eyes and the dangerous stirrings they created inside him. Friendship, that's all it was going to be, he insisted to himself. That's what he had to remember.

"He's here!" shouted Aimee, who'd been keeping watch by the front door. Before Lizzi could stop her, she'd bounded outside and got caught up in Pete's arms, as he swept her up into the air.

Both were grinning as they came into the house. Pete nodded to Lizzi. "Pete," she said in acknowledgment as he passed her a bottle of wine. She opened it and watched as he sat with Aimee and listened to her chatter with complete attention and interest.

She passed him a glass of wine and he shot her a quick, guarded smile before turning to Aimee again. She sat and marveled how well Pete and Aimee got along, considering they hadn't known each other long.

She'd thought, at Aimee's age, that she might have forgotten the afternoons spent doing homework and the walks along the lake shore at dusk with Pete. But it seemed she hadn't forgotten anything—not least her affection for him. And it also seemed that any firmness on Pete's side had had zero effect. Aimee liked him. More than liked him.

As she sipped her wine she realized she'd been wrong. Maybe, after Charles, she'd been *too* lenient with Aimee, in some ways trying to put right the wrongs that Charles had done. Maybe she had. And maybe it was time to put some firm boundaries in place for Aimee. Just as Pete had been doing. She'd got it wrong. What else had she got wrong?

"Time for bed, Aimee."

"Ah, Mum," Aimee wheedled. "Can't I stay up a little longer? Pete's only just arrived."

"No. You've had a long day. Get to bed, and I'll read you a quick story."

Aimee's bright eyes alighted on Pete. "Will you read me a story?"

"Aimee," Lizzi warned.

"If it's okay with your mum, I will," said Pete.

"Okay," she said, unable to resist Aimee's excitement. "Just make sure you choose a short book, Aimee. Call when you're in bed."

Aimee left the room and an awkward silence settled between Lizzi and Pete. Her gaze tangled with his and she looked away.

"So—"

"How—"

They spoke at once. He grinned, and she laughed.

"You first," said Pete. "You asked me here for a reason, so how about we cut to the chase, and you tell me what's on your mind?"

"Okay." She sucked in a deep breath. "I want to apologize. When you came around that last night, I panicked. You see, my ex, Charles, was really strict with Aimee." She paused, wondering how to go on, all the words she'd rehearsed suddenly failing her.

"How strict?" he asked quietly, his mouth tight, an uncharacteristic frown, sitting on his brow.

"I won't go into details, but it was enough that when I heard you being firm with her, I panicked. And then, when I realized you were also in the army, like Charles, I had a horrible sense of déjà vu—"

"What did he do, Lizzi? What did he do to you?"

She licked her lips. "I don't want to go into that."

"Was he 'strict' with you, too? Is that why you divorced him?"

She froze under Pete's fierce expression, and at the memories of just how "strict" Charles had been. She plucked her shirt sleeves down so they covered her burn marks but when she looked up she realized she'd been too late. He'd seen. He'd understood.

He rose and paced over to the window, looking out, away from her. His shoulders were tense and a muscle flickered in his jaw as he moved his head. "I can't bear the thought of either of you being hurt."

"I'm ready!" Aimee's call made them both turn around with a start.

Lizzi rose. "You don't have to go and read if you don't want to."

"It's fine; I want to." He took a deep breath and shook his head. "It'll take my mind off what you've told me."

The doors were open, and Lizzi listened as Pete settled himself into the easy chair at the foot of the bed and read Aimee her favorite story. There was no sign of anger in his tone, now. He'd managed to control it, something Charles had never been able to do.

She pushed aside the doors and walked out onto the deck, taking a nervous sip of wine. She hadn't told Pete much but he'd guessed the rest. Despite the fact he didn't know the full extent of it, she felt vulnerable and humiliated.

She didn't tell many people, only her close friends. Because, apart from wanting to keep Aimee from the truth, Charles's mother had lived near Shelter Springs until her recent death and hadn't the first idea about what Charles had done—about what he *could* do. And Lizzi had loved her, and didn't want to hurt her with the truth.

"She's nearly asleep already," Pete said as he picked up his glass and joined her on the deck.

"She's had a busy day."

He stood beside her, leaning against the wooden rail. They stood in companionable silence looking out across the lake toward the mountains, dark against the inky-blue night sky. "Thanks for telling me. I wondered what was up."

"I mean, it doesn't change things. I can't do relationships. I don't want one. But... you're moving into the area, and I wanted to clear the air."

He grunted and looked at her, his face mysterious in the darkness. "You want to be friends."

She licked her lips. "Yes."

The night thickened around them. The seconds passed, and a large moth batted against the outside lamp. Pete shrugged and raised his glass. "To friendship."

He leaned forward and tapped his glass against hers. He smiled and half-laughed.

"What?"

"Your eyes, Lizzi. Your eyes."

"What's wrong with them?"

"Nothing whatsoever. In fact, there are many things *right* with them. I'm laughing because you say friendship and your eyes tell me something else altogether."

"Eyes can't speak."

He huffed a brief laugh and goose-bumps bloomed where his breath warmed her skin. "Is that right?" he asked, as he gently touched her cheek. "They're speaking to me right now. You know? I've never seen eyes that change like yours."

She drew in a shaky breath. "Eyes don't change."

"Oh, they do. One minute they're the color of honey,

other times, like now, they're much darker, more like chocolate."

He licked his lips and smiled. "They're all signals, Lizzi. All showing me that you'd like to be more than friends with me. I can see it."

Lizzi had to summon all her willpower to move away from him. Only after she'd got the safety of a table between them did she turn to him. "I'm scared, Pete," she said, her voice barely a whisper.

"I know. I am, too."

He lifted his glass to hers once more. "Here's to... friendship and courage."

"Friendship," she repeated. Definitely friendship. But courage? Hadn't she been courageous enough, leaving Charles? Hadn't she been brave enough, bringing Aimee up on her own, without handouts from anyone? What more could be demanded of her? What more could she give? She shook her head.

"Courage," Pete repeated, his eyes fixed on hers, willing her to accept the challenge. For a challenge was exactly what it was.

She raised her glass to his but didn't repeat his words. She wasn't about to accept a challenge framed by anyone else. No, her only challenges in the future would be ones she set. No one else.

"To the future," she said. "Whatever it may bring."

His eyes narrowed as he clinked her glass. As they drank, she had the strange feeling that even though she hadn't accepted his toast, she'd be needing a whole lot of courage in the coming months.

CHAPTER FIVE

"Pinot noir, pinot gris, pinot blanc... we've the best cold climate wines in the region," said Steve, the owner of Tussock Hills Vineyard proudly.

"I don't doubt it," said Pete, as he lifted one of the pinot noir vines which grew vigorously in the harsh climate, as if his decision would depend on his inspection. Still smoothing the bright green leaves between his fingers he looked around at the small valley which sat thirteen hundred feet above sea level. Despite the fact it was the highest winery in New Zealand, it was obviously flourishing.

As Steve pointed out the different areas of the valley, Pete only half-listened. Instead, his eyes lifted to the mountains and stayed there. He might miss the Pacific Ocean on his doorstep, but he had a feeling the view of the Southern Alps, thrusting their brilliant snow-capped peaks into the bright blue sky, would soon take as strong a hold on him. *This* place was his home now. He'd felt an inkling of it when he, Max and their mates had first arrived at Shelter Springs. And his first run and swim had stirred his interest, and his heart, even further. And then there was Lizzi. How much of his feelings for his new home was about the place and how much about Lizzi, he couldn't have said. They were so intertwined he couldn't have separated out his feelings for one from the other if he'd tried.

"I reckon I'm going to miss this place," Steve said.

Pete cast a knowledgeable eye over the small hanging valley with its own microclimate in which grapevines only recently planted were already growing vigorously beside more established plantings. "I'm not surprised. You'll miss out on the fruits of your hard work. Not least in the house by the lake."

Steve tipped his hat and nodded, his weathered face barely betraying any emotion. "I'd be hanging on to it all myself if it weren't for the wife. She's determined to move closer to the kids and grandkids. Though where we're going to get a view like this in Christchurch, I don't know."

Pete shifted uneasily. The glimpse into Steve's family life brought back memories of his family, now all gone. Too many people gone—too many people gone before their time.

First Ellen, his childhood sweetheart, and then Alitia— his freedom-loving sister who'd refused his help or advice and had paid the consequences.

He suppressed the memories and walked over and took Steve's extended hand in a firm handshake. "Maybe. But you won't be wanting to look at the view when you have your family around you."

Steve smiled then for the first time. "True." They began to walk to the winery. "Got any family of your own?"

Pete shook his head as he looked around at the land he'd agreed to buy. "No. They're all dead."

"Sorry to hear that."

"Me, too."

"You'll have a family one day."

The sky was bright against Pete's narrowed eyes. "No plans for that. I've plenty of friends. They're my family." It was true, Pete thought. But it was also true that he'd like one particular friend to be closer than the others.

Steve gave a brief laugh. "I didn't have plans for a family and now look at me! Children and grandchildren everywhere! No, I've never found planning much use when it comes to women. They always seem to beat me to it. I *think* I know what's happening, *where* I'm going and then they spring something like this on me!"

"No one's going to spring anything on me," said Pete firmly.

Steve grinned. "Good luck with *that*."

Pete doubted luck would play any part in his desire to further his relationship with Lizzi. Just a whole lot of time to prove to her that they could be more than friends without compromising their independence.

Steve narrowed his eyes as they took one last look at the vineyard before turning to the winery buildings. "You might need luck with women, but you won't need luck with this lot."

"No. I can see that. I can also see Tussock Hills wines sitting comfortably with the best overseas wines. I've some export contacts who'll be very interested."

"Don't forget the domestic market. We're selling to all the big suppliers in the South Island, and we're beginning to pick up more orders in the North Island. They're taking as much as we can supply."

"Yeah, well, I might try a different tactic." Pete's research had already shown that re-pitching the wine to the higher end of the market and restricting its sale could achieve better prices.

"Good on you. I'll be watching your progress from the coast. I'm glad you wanted the house by the lake, too—it made the sale much simpler. The half-hour drive isn't so bad, and you've got the manager on site to keep a closer eye on things. Anyhow, let's go to the house and we'll seal the deal with a beer, the good old-fashioned Kiwi way."

Pete grinned. "Sounds great to me."

A few days later Pete cast a satisfied glance around the house of which he was the proud new owner. And not just the house. It seemed as well as wanting a quick sale, Steve's wife wanted to buy a completely new set of furniture for her beach house near Christchurch and had been more than happy for Pete to buy it all, lock, stock and barrel. And the barrels, Pete thought as he pictured them lined up in the cellar below, looked particularly interesting.

He walked out onto the imposing deck of the architecturally designed house overlooking the lake. It was situated some distance from the small township of Shelter Springs. But he didn't mind that. In fact he preferred not to have any neighbors; after all, that was what he was used to. Plus the fact that the curve of the lakeshore meant he got a good view of The Lakehouse Café in the distance, and Lizzi's house sitting snugly beside it. Just knowing Lizzi and Aimee were there made him feel good.

And knowing he'd be seeing them both soon, made him feel even better.

He walked through the house, its up-to-the minute textured concrete flooring warm from the sun. His mother would have liked it, he thought. Then he grunted. Who was he kidding? His mother loved the comfortable traditionally

designed and furnished home she'd shared with his father—
from the thick carpets, old-fashioned furniture and plenty
of family mementoes. There was none of that here. Nothing
personal.

Pete's happiness faltered a little and he looked out to the
mountain range. No, his mother would have been sad to see
Pete alone. She'd hated how he'd changed after Ellen had
passed away. Hated how he'd rarely brought the same girl
over to visit her twice. His mother had always said if he'd
planned his personal life as well as he'd organized his business life, she'd be happy. He sighed.

He picked up his keys, cast one more look around and
went outside into the heat of a summer's day in the
Mackenzie Country. His mother might not approve of his
life, but one thing his mother would most definitely have
approved of, was Lizzi.

―――――――

Lizzi listened to Gemma over the phone, as she prodded her
laptop desultorily. "No, no news yet." Lizzi leaned back in
her chair as Gemma continued to press money on her.

She looked up and saw Pete enter the café. She
smiled and beckoned him over. She'd heard that he'd been
around, settling himself into the community but she
hadn't seen him. Seemed he was being as good as his
word and not pushing her into giving more than she
wanted. Trouble was, she hardly knew herself what she
wanted.

He grinned and leaned against the door jamb, waiting
for her to finish the conversation.

"Got to go, now, Gemma. I'll catch you later."

"Sorry to interrupt," said Pete.

"You're not," said Lizzi. "In fact, you saved me from yet another lecture."

He frowned. "What about?"

"Oh, just about a loan I'm waiting to hear about."

He nodded, but didn't ask her anything further.

"Coffee?" she asked.

"Sure, thanks. So," he said, taking a stool by the coffee machine. "How are you?"

"I'm fine."

"No you're not," said Katie placing a new order beside the coffee machine. "You're stressed. Was that the bank on the phone?"

Lizzi shot Katie a warning look. "No."

"When were they meant to get back to you?"

Lizzi grimaced. "Yesterday at five pm. I've rung and left a message. I'll have to take another trip to Fairlie this afternoon if I don't hear. Everything will be closed by the end of the week for the long weekend."

"You do what you have to do. I'll take care of things here."

"Thanks, Katie. I appreciate it." She finished making the coffees and followed Pete to an outside table in the shade, overlooking the lake.

"So, are you going to tell me what you're stressed about?"

Lizzi sighed. She may as well tell him. "I'm waiting to hear from the bank about a loan."

"Hopefully, it can wait until next week because they finish up early tomorrow."

She frowned and looked away.

"Can it?" he asked.

She shook her head. "No."

"What's up? Anything I can help with?"

The fear and worry had been grinding away at her, worsening with each passing day. Suddenly the idea of offloading onto Pete was appealing. "Charles—my ex-husband—wants me to buy him out or he'll put the café on the market."

Pete's eyes blazed. "He'll do what?"

"He wants to sell. He wants to put all his money into his family's estate in Indonesia."

"But what about you? What about Aimee?"

"He doesn't care."

"Not about his own flesh and blood? Not about his little girl?"

Lizzi glanced around to make sure no one could over-hear, before shaking her head. "I'm doing what I can to keep it."

"But the bank *will* lend you the money, won't they?"

"I hope so. I'm waiting to hear."

"And, if they don't come through, are there any other options available to you?"

"No way. I'm doing this on my own, or not at all."

"But that's crazy. A simple loan will ensure your future."

"A simple loan will ensure I'm trapped and beholden to someone. I can't do that anymore."

He grunted and sat back in his chair.

"No, it's this way or not at all," Lizzi said. "I've a couple of days left. If I don't hear from them by tonight I'll go into Fairlie tomorrow."

Pete grunted and took a sip of his coffee. "So, are you working over the long weekend?"

"I can't. The café's open but it's the one time of year when I have to go home to Akaroa. We always go there for Waitangi weekend. It was Mum's birthday."

"Akaroa," said Pete. He looked away suddenly and Lizzi felt a sudden sadness.

"What are you doing for the holiday?"

He shrugged. "Settling in."

"No family?"

"No, no family. All dead."

"Oh..." Lizzi felt his emptiness, although he didn't say anything. The image of Akaroa, and her family's house on shores of Lantern Bay an hour out from Christchurch—with all its history and warmth and all her siblings—contrasted to the emptiness of Pete's weekend.

Pete finished his coffee and rose suddenly. "Hey, I'll pass on the cake. I've a few other things to get done today. I'll see you around."

"Sure." Lizzi frowned as she watched him leave. She rose slowly and joined Katie.

"He didn't stop for his cake," Katie said. "Was it the coffee?"

"No," said Lizzi, watching him take off down the road in his car. "I've a feeling it was something I said." She felt terrible. She'd described the members of her large family—who were as infuriating as they were lovable—and all the while he had no one. He had a beautiful home, but would be alone.

Once the thought had nudged its way into her brain she couldn't stop it. Her family always brought waifs and strays home for the holidays. Her sister Amber usually brought animals, but friends who were passing through and temporarily homeless, neighbors who were permanently homeless, they were all welcome at Belendroit. Sure, she wanted to be only friends, but that's what friends did, wasn't it? Made sure they weren't alone at holiday time.

Lizzi and Aimee were in the cottage when the roar of an engine made them both look out into the street. Aimee went running outside. "Uncle Pete!"

Pete handed a bag to Lizzi and high-fived Aimee who grabbed his hand and pulled him in to show him her latest computer game.

Lizzi's breath caught at the sound of her daughter's laughter and she followed them into the cottage.

She placed the bag on the table. "What have you got here?" She pulled out a bottle of Moet. "Expecting to celebrate?"

He glanced up from Aimee's game. "Every day's a celebration. Isn't it, Aimee?"

She smiled doubtfully. "Maybe."

"No *maybe* about it. I bet you did great at school today. How was English?"

Her face brightened. "Miss Taylor said my story was wonderful." Her face flushed at the memory and she proceeded to describe the details of her story.

"Excellent!"

"And what do *I* have to celebrate?" asked Lizzi.

"Great company?" Pete offered.

Lizzi's cell phone rang and she pounced on it. "Hello? Yes, speaking." She listened as the bank manager waffled on for a few moments before coming to the point. She pressed the speaker phone.

"We're agreed. You can have the loan. We've dealt with all the paperwork at today's meeting, so all you have to do, Mrs. Burnett—"

She jumped up and punched the air silently. "Lizzi,

please. Call me Lizzi." She might have kept Burnett for Aimee's sake, but hated hearing it.

"*Lizzi*, is to do as you promised. Increase the turnover by twenty percent and all will be well."

"I certainly will. Thank you. Thank you so much."

She clicked the phone off and tossed it onto the table, throwing her hands in the air. "Mummy did it, baby! Mummy did it all by herself. No more going cap in hand to anyone, we're on our own!"

"Is that a good thing, Mummy?"

"Sure is, baby. We're in control of our own destiny. No one else is."

Aimee grinned and jumped off the chair and punched the air. "Mummy did it!" Lizzi took her hands and twirled her around the room. Laughing they fell into one of the armchairs by the picture window and Lizzi gave Aimee a big hug.

When she looked up, Pete was standing watching them with a big grin on his face. "Look at you two! Like a couple of kids."

"I *am* a kid," said Aimee indignantly.

"Well, that's a good point. But what about your mum?"

"She's just happy 'cos she did it." Aimee frowned.

"Another good point. Why the frown, Aimee?"

"What is it you did, Mummy?"

Lizzi and Pete looked at each other and burst into laughter, as Pete popped the cork on the Moet.

"I've done it, Pete! I've built a wall to save my princess!" said Aimee, fiddling with the computer Pete had rigged up in the back of the car. It was a three hour drive from Shelter

Springs to Akaroa and Lizzi had learned from long experience that it was easier if Aimee was occupied.

"Cool. Well done. Now you need to make sure that she has enough supplies to keep her going."

Lizzi tried to focus on her laptop. The marketing emails she was writing were even more important now the loan had been confirmed. Because now she had exact figures and firm deadlines to meet each month.

"Oh," said Aimee, after a long pause. "How do I do that?"

As Lizzi continued to write emails and check over figures on her laptop, she half-listened while Pete explained the intricacies of the computer game. As he got more involved, Lizzi looked up at him. He was focused on the road ahead as they left the Mackenzie high country and emerged onto the flat Canterbury Plains. And yet he seemed to have a firm mental grip on Aimee's game.

"How on earth do you know all this stuff?"

"Same way you know about baking, I guess. By doing it."

"What, you spent your nights on Waiheke Island playing computer games?"

"Remember Susie?"

Lizzi nodded. "I remember you talking about her. She worked with you, right? Had a son?"

"That's Susie. Well, where she lived was pretty isolated, and when her son, Tom, came home from school, the least I could do was to keep him company. We'd go fishing sometimes and play a few computer games. He taught me everything I know."

That figured. Lizzi smiled to herself and looked at her spreadsheet. Pete's ease with kids somehow made her feel safe.

He glanced at her. "You should try it sometime."

"What?"

"Chilling out. Relaxing. Playing a few games."

"I *do* relax!"

"No, you don't." He glanced in the rear vision mirror. "Does she, Aimee?"

Aimee looked up from the computer and screwed up her face in thought. "She does when she's asleep."

Pete laughed. "You see? You need to try relaxing while you're *awake*. Like now, for instance. You need to stop studying"—he glanced down to see what she was looking at —"spreadsheets and start... chatting."

"Chatting? About what?"

"*There*, right *there*, is where you're going wrong. You see, the idea of chatting is that it doesn't necessarily have a point."

"Everything has to have a point. Otherwise it's a waste of time."

"You're wrong, Elizabeth."

"Don't call me Elizabeth. It reminds me of being told of by Dad. And..." She trailed off, not wanting to mention her ex.

"Put your laptop away and I won't."

She grunted but reluctantly closed her laptop, her fingers hooking over its smooth, cool edges as if holding on to it for support. "Okay. I'm all yours. What shall we talk about?"

"How about filling me in on your family. Who will be there? I haven't heard from Max for a while."

"I'm not sure if Max will be there. The Queenstown resort is eating up a good bit of his time."

"Hm. Like brother, like sister."

"That's true. He's the eldest, and then me, and we're

most alike. Rachel will be there, but not Rob. He's overseas. And Amber will be there—she never misses an opportunity to be with family. Cameron's never there—none of us have seem him in ages. But we'll see Gabe; he's started his practice in Akaroa. And the others will come and go."

"You're very lucky."

"In what way?"

"To have so many brothers and sisters and cousins that you don't even name them all. That you can include them all under the umbrella term of 'the others'."

"Hm. I hadn't thought of it like that. I guess you're right. They're all different, but I love them all. Even if some of them are more challenging. Like Dad." She shook her head.

"From what you've told me about him, you're probably like him. That's why you don't get on so well."

"I am *not*."

"He made his fortune in property development, didn't he?"

"Yes. Mainly in Christchurch."

"I bet he never relaxed, too."

She sent him an irritated look. He was spot on. But she still didn't like to think she resembled her father who questioned everything in her life—from her career choice to her divorce from a war hero who was respected and revered across the nation.

"No, he didn't." She sighed. "And I shouldn't be either. I should be at the café, trying to drum up business and keep what I already have."

"You've got good staff to cover for you. There's nothing more you can do by being there."

"No, but I can work now. I'm worried I won't make the repayments unless I have everything planned within an inch of its life."

"And you have, so don't worry. You've got those overseas weddings coming up. They'll set you up well. And those people will return to their countries, tell other people what a fantastic location and what fantastic food and service they received, and then all their friends will return to get married, and honeymoon after that. Basically, you're set for life."

Lizzi nodded slowly, her mind revolving over all the aspects of managing the events, as well as the daily routine customers. "Yes, it should be fine."

He reached over and took her hand and squeezed it. "It *will* be fine. You'll *make* it fine."

She gazed out at the lush pastures and established farms of the Canterbury Plains. "But what if I don't?" She grimaced, turned to face him and lowered her voice. "What if something happens and I can't make payments? We'll have to..." She glanced at Aimee who was oblivious to everything around her except her game.

"It won't happen. I know it won't happen."

She scoffed. "No one can know for sure."

Pete didn't reply.

"I've *got* to make it work, Pete. I've spent my whole life being pushed and pulled by other people. First by my father and then"—another quick glance at Aimee who was singing out of key to something on her noise-canceling headphones —"and then Charles. It's time I took control—for Aimee's sake as well as my own."

She glanced up at Pete whose eyes were narrowed in concentration as he overtook a campervan. His handsome face, with its open features, looked more closed now, lines of tension around his mouth which she hadn't noticed before. The intermittent shadows caused by the high trees that lined the fields made his face look different somehow, and she had a sudden notion she was looking at the face of a stranger.

Fear rose from nowhere, eating at her inside. She looked away, willing it to subside. But it didn't completely. Didn't she once believe she knew Charles well? She swallowed hard. She'd thought she'd known him all those years ago but, in the end, he'd changed into someone she didn't know. Was there more to Pete than she'd imagined? She suddenly realized how little she knew him.

The trees had given way to a more expansive sun-soaked landscape. She glanced up at Pete, and he met her gaze with an open smile. He was Pete once more. But she frowned as the feeling continued and she looked out the window toward the sea, hidden behind rolling hills, where her home town lay. Akaroa. Despite the sunshine, a distant haze lay on the horizon.

She had to be careful—not only about her business, but with the men in her life. She refused to be controlled, refused to be owned and used anymore.

As they drove over the hills from Christchurch toward Akaroa Harbor, they caught the first glimpses of the water through the trees which lined the road. The tide was out and the water, pooled on the undulating mudflats, shone silver. Further out, the sea was calm and reflected the golden hills and the green trees which fringed the shoreline opposite. A haze still lingered on the horizon, not threatening now but as soft as a sable-haired brushstroke along the blue-gray of the sea.

Aimee leaned forward, craning her neck to see out the front window. "Are we there?"

"Not yet. Akaroa is beyond those hills."

"Oh," she sighed. "It's a long way."

"It's only another ten minutes."

Lizzi reached for Aimee's hand and stroked it. Aimee leaned her head against Lizzi's arm. "Are you looking forward to seeing your bedroom again?"

Aimee sat up in excitement. "Yes! Even though I only visit, Grandad said it's mine and would always be ready for me. Do you think the toys Grandad gave me will still be there?"

"I *know* they'll still be there. And, knowing your aunties and uncles, there will probably be more."

Aimee sat back, looking out the window, lost in thought.

Pete exchanged a smile with Lizzi. "Will I have toys in my bedroom?"

She tapped his leg with the back of her hand. "You have enough toys. Like this car."

"You have to admit it's comfortable."

"Yes, I guess I do." Which was the problem. Pete made her world so much more comfortable, so much more enjoyable for just being in it. And she didn't want that. She couldn't trust that. Not yet.

Pete glanced up at the beautifully preserved colonial houses which climbed the steep hills above the bay. "Akaroa sure is a beautiful place."

Lizzi looked across the gleaming stretch of water to the rumpled hillside on the far side of the harbor, whose ridges were bright in the sun, and whose green-lined gullies lay in the shadows, and tried to imagine it through a stranger's eyes. They'd passed through the center of Akaroa, and their view of the water was hidden by a rocky, tree-topped promontory—owned by her family—at the end of which they turned onto a rough track which would lead to the secluded bay which was all their own—Lantern Bay.

"Yes, it is. I suppose you take it for granted when you grow up in a place."

"It must have been an idyllic childhood."

"As idyllic as most people's I guess. Big family, lots of arguments, but lots of love, too."

"And you had the bay to yourselves, too," piped up Aimee.

"Yes, we had the bay."

Pete turned into a drive beside a white-painted gate, which hadn't been closed in Lizzi's memory and was now embedded in the branches of a tree. They bumped their way along the pot-holed drive, around a stand of trees and parked to one side of the house.

"The house is still smiling!" shouted Aimee.

"It doesn't stop smiling when we leave." Lizzi understood perfectly. If houses had expressions, Belendroit's was one of charming innocence, surprise almost, with the roofs over the windows that jutted out either side, like raised eyebrows. You simply wanted to look after it. Between the two wings of the house lay the veranda, deep and shady, full of white cane furniture and green plants, the main room of the house in summer. On both sides of the house, lanterns hung, lit despite the fact it was broad daylight.

"Looks like there's a full house already," said Pete.

She followed Pete's gaze and saw the cars. Her brothers must have arrived. And then she noticed a rusting yellow mini; her youngest sister, Amber, had also arrived. Rachel, who was staying the summer at Belendroit, was the first to spot them.

"Aimee!" She gave Aimee a big hug before Aimee went running off to see her uncles. "Hey, big sis!" Rachel gave

Lizzi a kiss before looking at Pete. "And you've brought your man. Heya, Pete!"

Before Lizzi could correct Rachel, Pete and Rachel were walking up to the house, chatting easily as if they were long-lost friends. As Lizzi followed them up to the house, ducking her head to avoid the branches from which late fragrant blossoms dripped onto the path, she hoped that the rest of her family wouldn't make the same mistake.

"Elizabeth! And you must be Pete! Good to see you both." Her father greeted them with his usual aristocratic aloofness. While her father chatted with Pete, Lizzi leaned over the veranda to check on Aimee, who was playing Frisbee with Amber and the dogs. Then the French windows opened and her brothers stepped onto the veranda to greet them.

"Lizzi!" The shouts went up as her brothers came and embraced her. She was so caught up in the chaos of family hugs and teasings that she didn't notice the warmth of the welcome they gave Pete.

"About time Lizzi got herself a new man. Welcome, Pete!" said Gabe.

Pete grinned at Lizzi's frustrated expression but didn't say anything to correct her younger brother, Gabe.

"Gabe," Lizzi said, hoping he'd pick up on her warning tone. "Pete is my friend. *Only* my friend."

Gabe grinned. "Yeah, right. Whatever you say."

Frustrated, she confronted Max, older than her by only a year. He stood a little apart, assessing her through narrowed eyes. Max had always taken it upon himself to care for his many siblings, including her.

"Lizzi." He nodded to Lizzi with characteristic restraint.

"Max, how have you been keeping?"

"Fine."

"How's the Queenstown resort going?"

"Better than I'd imagined. The café?"

Lizzi shrugged as she accepted a drink from her father who continued to talk with Pete.

"It's all mine now. Charles wanted out."

Max grunted but never took that intense gaze from Lizzi. "Yours? What? Bank loan?"

"Yep."

He thrust his fingers through his hair. "Lizzi! I told you to come to me. I said I'd sort it if the moment came. Whatever interest you're paying, it'll be over the top."

"I know, Max, but I wanted to do it on my own this time. And I did."

"For goodness sake, Lizzi. I've beaten down the most hard-nosed businessmen in Australasia on different deals, and none of them have got the better of me. None, except you. Reckon I've met my match with you."

A slow smile spread over his face and despite his admonishment, she could see he was proud of her. Lizzi couldn't help softening. Her big brother might pry, he might give her a hard time, but she knew he'd always love her and look out for her, just as he did with everyone around him.

"Reckon you have."

"Got the same genes as Dad."

The smile vanished. "Dad? You reckon?" How was it that twice, in the same morning, she'd been likened to the man with whom she'd always had a difficult relationship?

"Yeah, of course. The others are more like Mum. Now, Mum could always get to the bottom of whatever mischief we kids got up to... *and* Dad got up to." He cast a narrowed glance at his father.

"Until we got older and wiser that is."

"*Did* you get wiser, sis?"

"Don't start."

He grinned and pulled her to him and gave her a quick hug. Just like his nature, his embraces were intense, and all-encompassing. And, also like the rest of him, you missed them when they were gone. Because at that moment you felt the vital spirit of the man which he hid from the rest of the world.

"Truce." He pulled away. "Now go and see that man of yours."

Lizzi looked with alarm at Pete who was charming her two sisters and father. "Pete is *not* my man. He's a friend."

"Don't sound so indignant. It's an easy mistake to make."

She took a long slug of wine, willing the alcohol to relax her. "I don't see why."

"You don't? How about the fact he's sold up his business interests on Waiheke Island, and he's moved to Shelter Springs."

She shrugged. "He was in talks with the Tussock Hills owner before I met him. He wanted a change."

"Right," Max said, humoring her, but obviously not believing her. "Well, whatever. He's a good bloke."

She glanced once more at Pete as he let out a loud whoop and caught Aimee in his arms.

"Aimee and Pete look to be getting on well."

Lizzi kept her lips firmly closed as she tried to suppress her temper at her prying brother. Max never beat around the bush, unfortunately. "Yes, as you can see."

A Frisbee flew into Max's leg. He picked it up and looked around.

"Sorry!" shouted Amber, who was playing with the two cocker spaniels who were as crazy as she was.

"You will be!" shouted Max, who threw it straight back at her.

Lizzi left them to it and walked up behind Pete and hesitated, listening to Aimee chatter away to Pete, and Gabe, who also lived in Akaroa, and Rachel, who lived in Wellington.

There was a tap on the shoulder. "Another drink, Elizabeth?" her father asked, holding up a bottle of white wine. "Thought we should celebrate. All you kids together. Happens so rarely. Just wish..." His voice trailed off as he looked away toward what had been Jonny's—their youngest brother's—room.

Lizzi reached out and touched his arm. "We all wish Jonny and Mum were still with us."

Lizzi's father took a sharp intake of breath. "No doubt they're here in spirit, as your mother would say. But what with Max"—he glanced at Max who was calming the two dogs with a word—"and you both always away."

The barb was aimed squarely at her and Max. She felt a wave of guilt. She smiled briefly. "It's pretty busy at the moment at the café."

He poured her a glass of wine and looked up at her from under bushy white eyebrows, his blue eyes, eagle bright. "You work too hard."

Another dig. She swallowed her irritation. "I have to, Dad. Have to look after Aimee."

He shook his head. "I'll never understand why you divorced Charles. With his money, you could have taken things easy."

"I'm *not* a gold digger."

"I didn't say you were, darling, but you must admit that, to an outsider, your marriage appeared pretty darned perfect."

She tried to smile with gritted teeth, but doubted she'd succeeded. "Key word, Dad. 'Appeared.'"

"Well, if you'd confided in me perhaps I could have understood your decision."

"Perhaps you could." She nodded emphatically, still trying desperately to control her irritation. "And perhaps you couldn't. But, as I tried to explain at the time, it's personal."

"I'm sorry... I didn't mean to rake over old ground. Forgive a foolish old man."

Lizzi shook her head, defeated. He always did this, drove in a knife with one hand, and charmed you with the other. "You are neither foolish, nor old, but I forgive you anyway."

"Well, I'm sure it's more than I deserve," he said in a tone which clearly showed that he didn't believe his own words. Her father was born believing he deserved the best and didn't rest until everything was as he liked it. And both Max and Pete believed she was like him? Goodness, she hoped not. "Drink up, darling."

She took a sip of the wine. "Um, this is nice. What is it?"

Her father nodded in the direction of Pete. "Courtesy of Pete's Whisper Creek Winery. All sold up now, I believe." He cocked a knowing eye at Lizzi. Her father held the wine up to the light revealing the delicate shade of green. "Tastes of lemons and grass. Beautiful. So, are you going to tell me why he sold up?"

She sighed. Seemed all her family had put two and two together and made five. "Because, because..."

"It was time to move on," Pete said as he approached them.

They both looked up to see Pete standing there. Lizzi wondered how much he'd heard.

"Must have been hard to leave the winery behind, Pete. Because this wine is beautiful," her father said.

"Yes, it was hard but as I say, it was time to move on. I'd been based on Waiheke Island most of my life, but with my parents and sister gone, there was no reason to stay anymore. Besides I left it in good hands. Susie practically ran the place in the end, and it was bought by James Mackenzie. I didn't realize they were old friends. And it looks like he'll be staying there longer and having a more 'hands-on' interest in it than I first thought. So it might work out for both of them," he said with a smile.

"And for you?" Her father rocked back on his heels, one hand thrust in the smart stone-colored chinos he always wore, the other cradling the glass. He was born to a patriarchal role, Lizzi thought with a smile. "You reckon things will work out for you here?" asked her father, with his usual lack of tact.

Pete grinned. "I'm working on it. I've bought a new winery half an hour out from Shelter Springs and a house by the lake. They were both owned by the same couple."

Her father touched Pete's arm. "I'm glad." He looked out toward Aimee. "Now I'm off to see my only granddaughter. I don't know what's got into my lot. Eight kids and only one of them has given me a grandchild... and I don't get to see enough of her."

Lizzi rolled her eyes as she watched her father take Amber's position behind Aimee, who was now on the old swing, and give her a gentle push up into the sky, the old rope creaking against the branch of the oak tree.

"You've got a great family, Lizzi," said Pete.

"Great at winding me up!" said Lizzi. But, despite what

she said, her heart warmed to see her normally shy daughter, blossoming under the attention of her family.

"You don't seem to mind too much." Pete held up his glass to the sunlight. "Even the wine seems to like it over here. The light's different, softer, more subtle. It's brought out a different set of flavors." He swirled it in the sunlight and Lizzi couldn't take her eyes off his fingers—long, strong and tanned as they enclosed the glass like a lover. Like they'd done to her until she'd called a halt. Her skin prickled as if his fingers, which trailed over the condensation on the wine glass, were instead trailing over her sensitive skin. She swallowed and looked up and saw he was looking at her carefully. "Seems everything is a little different here, in this coastal light. Even you."

She shook her head, and her ponytail swung. "No... I'm just the same."

"No, you're more vulnerable here. In the Mackenzie Country you're always so capable, so in control of everything, so strong—"

"You make me sound inhuman."

"No, not inhuman. Definitely not inhuman. In fact, very human—it's like you feel the need to fight to keep the world away from you and Aimee."

She focused on the distant dark hills. "Sometimes it feels that way. Even, here, at Belendroit."

He followed her glance toward her father. "But they're fights with people you love, and who love you."

She turned to him, realizing he was right. He was looking at her with an intense expression, his whole focus on her. As if he were looking into her soul and understanding her. Even her husband had never seemed interested in doing that.

"Maybe you're right. But I'm not good with love. Always seem to push it away."

"No, Lizzi. It's control you're not good with. Not love, I'm sure you're just fine with love."

"Are you? I wish I could believe that."

He smiled that sexy smile and her heart missed a beat. He stepped away. "You will. When you're ready."

She wished he hadn't stepped away. "And when will that be?"

"Soon, I hope." He flashed her a warm grin and began to walk down the steps to the garden. He stopped suddenly and turned to her. "You can have love without control, you know. They don't have to go together. Relationships don't require either party to be dependent on the other. At least I hope not."

He disappeared under the spreading branches of the pohutukawa tree from which lanterns hung.

She hoped so too.

CHAPTER SIX

The veranda at Belendroit, which overlooked Lantern Bay, was large and sheltered by a thick wisteria vine which had witnessed countless family dinners. The old table, with its worn knots and silvered wood, was laden with the different dishes they'd all brought with them.

Since her mother had died, the Sunday dinner on the long holiday weekend had evolved into a potluck lunch which ensured there was something for everyone—from vegan food for Amber through to hearty meat dishes for the boys—all contained in the eclectic mix of antique china her mother loved to collect.

When, as a child, Lizzi had asked her once why she didn't collect complete services, just oddments, her mother had replied with an amused look. "Where would the fun be in that?"

And that about summed up her quirky mother. She was all about fun, about being spontaneous. She'd only had to enter a room for the atmosphere to lighten and for laughter to begin.

Her sister Amber had inherited their mother's fun side.

She didn't have a full-time job, nor two cents to rub together, and yet she didn't seem to be aware that this should *not* make her happy. Because she was.

Lizzi felt a tiny pang of envy when she saw the appropriately named Amber, with her long red hair, telling a rambling, and no doubt imaginative, story to Pete. Amber was an artist, and she wove stories with her words, as well as her paintbrush. Completely unself-conscious, completely in a world of her own.

A small smile settled on Pete's lips as he listened to Amber, and his eyes were creased in that ever-ready smile that always got to Lizzi. It always made her want to smile. She had a sudden thought that Pete might be interested in Amber. Because, for one thing, who wouldn't be? And for another, Lizzi had made it clear she only wanted to be friends. But despite what she'd said she felt a twist of something like jealousy in her gut.

But then Pete turned and caught her eye, and his expression changed—it warmed and caressed her. She smiled as if caught out. She looked at her plate and stirred a mixture of unappealing beans and carrots—no doubt Amber's offering—and wished she were someone different, someone without a past which had left its indelible mark on her, someone who could trust.

She continued to listen as everyone around her shared stories and laughter, wishing her mother was here. She would have made everything all right. Lizzi had been able to talk to her about anything. She would have known what to do about Charles. But she'd passed away seven years before, shortly after Charles and Lizzi had married, so she never knew what he was really like. Lizzi was glad that her mother hadn't had to experience the heartache of her younger brother Jonny's death. He'd died while overseas only six months before, and the grief was still too raw to discuss openly.

Suddenly she was aware of silence around the table. She looked up to see everyone looking at her.

"Isn't it, Lizzi?" said Pete, with a raised eyebrow, obviously repeating himself.

"What? Sorry? I was miles away."

"I was saying that February is going to be a big month for The Lakehouse Café."

Lizzi widened her eyes. Apart from Max, her family rarely showed any interest in her business. "Yes, I've bookings for weddings throughout February. And March." She paused, waiting to see if her family's eyes had glazed over yet, but all eyes were still on her, so she kept on talking.

Pete relaxed in his chair. He'd got her talking at last. And, more to the point, he'd got her family listening. *Really* listening.

He frowned. He didn't quite understand what was going on here, what the dynamics of this family were. *His* family had always been quite straightforward, but not the Connellys. Nothing was at it seemed with them. No doubt because they were all distinctive characters with minds of their own. And, in some cases, those minds were very much at odds with each other. But, strangely, it didn't appear to stop them from loving each other.

"And it seems the Japanese couple who were married on the Lakehouse dock last month have spread the word," he prompted at a lull in the conversation.

"Yes," Lizzi continued. "They're bringing their whole family next week and have booked out our function room for a couple of days."

Max leaned forward. "You're doing great, Lizzi. I'm real proud of what you're doing, and how you're doing it all on your own. Awesome." He nodded as he sat back in his chair, his eyes never leaving his blushing sister.

Good old Max, thought Pete. The other siblings meant well, but Max really understood Lizzi.

"You're so lucky, Lizzi." Amber pulled her feet up on the cane chair and hugged her knees, as Pete and Max talked.

Lizzi gave her sister a wry grin. "Lucky? In what way? Sometimes I feel that 'luck' only ever gives me a casual glance before passing me by."

"How can you say that? You've got Aimee, you're a whizz at business, your café is thriving, and you've loads of friends."

"Yeah, and I'm grateful and love all of that. But I'm not sure what role luck plays in it."

"You work hard. I get that."

"You don't sound very happy. What's up?"

Amber shrugged. "I need to get away from here for a while."

"Man troubles?"

Amber rolled her eyes. "Big time. But I've no money to get away."

"Then why don't you come to Shelter Springs for a while? I need the help at the café and with Aimee. I was going to advertise for live-in staff when I got home. Do you want the job? Basically some waitressing at unsociable hours and some babysitting duties. The rest of the time you could paint. How about it?"

Amber's eyes opened wide. "Really? You mean it?"

The more Lizzi thought about it, the more she realized what a brilliant idea it was. "Sure. It would be great."

"That's fabulous." Amber hopped off the chair and gave Lizzi a big hug. "You're a wonderful sister, Lizzi! Come on, let's go and tell Aimee."

They walked outside. The light was only just beginning to fade in the long southern twilight and the hum of conversations, punctuated by the odd burst of laughter, drifted up from the beach, along with the smell of an open fire.

Lizzi shivered. "You go, Amber. I'll come and join you in a minute. I want to grab a wrap."

Lizzi returned inside the sprawling old house where secrets and treasures revealed themselves in every corner. It was huge but warm and welcoming, furnished with lush materials, velvets, full of books inherited from her mother's family who'd been among the original French settlers on the peninsula. Lizzi loved this style of decorating—so instinctive and personal—and only now realized that it exactly reflected the way she'd decorated the café. It made her feel good—made her feel closer to the mother she'd lost too soon. She might have inherited her father's business sense, but it seemed she'd also inherited a few traits from her mother.

Her mother's things still lay all around, even after seven years. She picked up an Indian paisley shawl which lay across a spindle-backed chair and pulled it around her shoulders. She went outside and stood for a few moments watching the others, thinking she was alone.

"Catherine?" she heard her father say in a wondering tone.

She looked around and saw him sitting at the far end of the veranda, alone.

"Dad! I didn't see you there. What did you say?"

"I never saw it before."

She walked up to her father and for the first time thought that he was looking older. It made her sad.

"Saw what?"

"How like your mother you are."

Strange that he should voice her thoughts. "The shawl, I guess."

"No, it's more than that."

"Mind if I join you?" she asked.

Her father sat in the white-painted wicker chair and looked up at Lizzi. "Be my guest."

She came and stood beside his chair, rested her arms on the veranda railing, and looked toward the beach where the others were gathered.

He rested his head on the hand-appliqued cushion and eyed her intently. "So how long are you staying, Elizabeth?"

"Just another night. I have to get back to the café."

"Of course."

A shriek pierced the air. She tensed. "That's Aimee. I hope she's okay. I'll go—"

"Let her be. The family will look after her. You're too protective of that child."

Lizzi frowned. "I've had to be. I'm a single parent."

"And that was your choice."

"Yep!" Lizzi peered into the violet night, watching Aimee being swung around by Max. "My choice," she said between gritted teeth. Everyone blamed her for her divorce from one of New Zealand's war heroes. Apart from Max and a few close friends, no one knew why she'd left the handsome, courageous, rich Kiwi boy. And that was the way it was going to have to stay. She owed Charles's mother that much, and hoped Aimee's bad memories would soon fade, and be replaced by the image of a war hero.

She heard her father sigh behind her. "No doubt you

had your reasons, whatever they were. Same damn reasons that makes you slave away in that café of yours." He grunted.

"You'll have to face it, Dad. I'm never going to be the daughter you hoped I'd be."

The cane squeaked as he rose heavily from the chair and came up to her and gripped her arms with a strength she hadn't known him to possess. "You've got it wrong, girl. I only want an easier life for you. I'm proud of you... of course I am."

"Why exactly?"

He opened his mouth to speak but paused too long.

"Yeah, right. You're proud of me, but you just can't think why, eh Dad?" She reached out and deadheaded some roses which had withered too soon. "You need to water these plants."

"You know I'm no good with plants. That was your mother's area of expertise."

"Yeah, she was a nurturer, all right."

"Just like you." Their gaze met.

"Like me? Everyone says I'm like you."

"You're like your mother, not only in looks, but in all the important ways."

She smiled and turned away. They'd formed some kind of truce. At least for the time being.

"Now go and join the others. Have some fun."

Lizzi kissed her father's cheek and walked through the overgrown garden. She ducked under the spreading pohutukawa tree, strung with lanterns whose lights could be seen from Akaroa, and continued down to the sandy bay, drawn by the snap and crackle of the flames teasing their way deep into the driftwood in the fire pit. Pete stood next to Max with a beer in hand, while the others sat around the fire. She was drawn to Pete but stopped short.

"Hey, sis, what have you been doing?" asked Max after a quick look from one to the other.

"Talking to Dad." Gabe handed her a beer, and she unscrewed the top.

"Good."

She looked at Max. "Why?"

"He worries about you."

"You have to be kidding."

"No, I can see it in his eyes. He's worried and he doesn't know what to do to make things right for you."

"Saying something supportive and nice might be a start."

"Yeah, well, maybe he doesn't know where to begin." Max glanced at Pete. "I'm off to wind Amber up."

Lizzi sat on the sand, and leaned against the side of an upturned dinghy, just outside the circle of firelight. Pete sat beside her.

"Thanks for inviting me, Lizzi. I realize you probably did it out of selfless pity for someone alone during a holiday weekend. And I'm afraid I accepted it out of a selfish desire to hang out with you and your family."

Lizzi paused. Why exactly had she invited him? "No, really, I thought it would be—"

"It's okay," Pete interrupted. "Whatever impulse made you extend the invitation, it's all right by me."

He looked straight ahead, over the flames toward where Max, Amber, Rachel and Gabe sat, laughing at some family joke.

"I miss that," Pete said.

"What?"

Pete indicated the group the other side of the fire pit

with his beer bottle. "That closeness. The familiarity. The short-hand family uses, knowing that the others will understand. It's a solid foundation of love which you take for granted until it's gone."

Pete rested his head against the dinghy, still looking straight ahead, his profile lit by the darting flames, the shadows they created revealing more of his strength than the most brilliant light could have done.

"I'm sorry," she said, wincing at the lameness of her response. She couldn't think of any words that could convey how much she understood and felt his pain. "And thank you for showing me what's in front of me, but which I hardly notice. I get so wrapped up in my own things. Aimee, the café, money..."

He turned to her then. "I don't notice *you* anywhere on that list."

She gave a brief laugh. "I guess I got left off so long ago I can't remember me being there."

"Then maybe you should add yourself. To the top, I reckon."

"I'm a mother," she said softly. "My child will always be at the top of my list."

As if on cue, Aimee left her position within Rachel's arms and stumbled over to Lizzi. "I'm tired, Mum," said Aimee, yawning, as she fell into Lizzi's lap.

Lizzi put her arms around Aimee and pulled her tight against her in a big hug. Aimee nestled into Lizzi's embrace, and Lizzi kissed the top of her head as Aimee yawned. She pulled the shawl from around her shoulders and covered Aimee who snuggled under its warmth. And there, at that moment, Lizzi realized the truth of Amber's words. She *was* lucky. And, she realized the truth of Pete's words. It didn't matter what else happened, she'd always have her family.

"Lizzi, what's up? Are you crying?" whispered Pete, his head close to hers. She pursed her lips and nodded, unable to stop the tears from falling down her cheeks, as both hands still held the now sleeping Aimee.

Pete brought his finger against her cheek and swept the tears away. He put his arm around her, and she leaned against him. None of her siblings seemed to notice anything was different. None of them looked at them askance. There were no raised eyebrows, or grins, to question her earlier assertions that Pete and she were just friends. They simply didn't appear to notice. Maybe they'd all got it right, mused Lizzi, and it was *her* that was slow on the uptake. Because being in the arms of Pete Marshall sure felt right.

It was gone midnight when Lizzi made herself a warm drink and stepped onto the veranda. Beyond the soft glow of the lantern, an inky darkness spread all around and the deep silence of the night was only punctuated by the occasional soft hooting of a morepork owl and the lapping of the water on the beach. Despite the sound of the water, and haunting cries of the nocturnal birds, it felt different to the stillness of the Mackenzie Country.

She heard the door open and someone step outside. She knew who it was even before he spoke. He came and leaned on the rail, beside her.

"You like my family," she said with a smile.

"I *love* your family."

She nodded and took a sip of her hot chocolate. "You looked like you were getting on well with Amber at dinner."

He chuckled. "Who wouldn't get on well with Amber? She's adorable."

Lizzi grunted, totally dissatisfied by his answer and

looked the other way, toward the blackness of the trees. "She's coming to stay in Shelter Springs for a while."

"That'll be nice for you and Aimee."

"And you." She couldn't help probing.

He touched her neck gently with his finger, drawing it up and hooking a lock of her hair away from her face, carefully placing it on her back. "There, now I can see the profile of the woman I can't stop thinking about."

She turned sharply to face him. "Even though I said the things I said?"

He shrugged. "You showed me you were scared, but not disinterested. But maybe I got that wrong. Are you disinterested? Because if you are, I'll leave it at that. I'll be gone and won't bother you again."

She shook her head. "I'm not disinterested, just cautious, just don't want to see history repeating itself. Just wary."

He nodded. "Wary is okay. *I'm* wary. I don't want to get married for years—if ever. I don't want to stop traveling, stop doing what I want to do. And I don't want to stop anyone I'm involved with from doing the same."

"Then I'm surprised you can't stop thinking about me!"

"Thinking about you, wanting to be with you—none of those things have anything to do with wanting to settle down. I'd thought you'd have appreciated the difference. *Celebrated* the difference, in fact."

She did. But why did she, at the same time, feel put out? "Yes," she said slowly. "You're right. A relationship which doesn't try to trap me is appealing."

"Good. Now, why don't you tell me what those tears were about earlier."

She looked away. "Ah, I'd hoped you might have forgotten about them."

"No way. Look at me, Lizzi." She sighed and did as he asked. "Tell me."

"It's hard to put into words."

"Try, because I'm not good at guessing."

"Okay. I suppose it's the first time in an awful long time that everything's felt... right."

"Because Aimee was in your arms and you were surrounded by your family?"

She smiled. "Partly. But it was also something else. You see, I usually sit where I sat, watching the others." She shrugged. "I don't know why. Habit. I'm more of an introvert than the others; I like my own space. The downside of that is I often feel alone, even with my family. But tonight, for the first time I didn't feel alone. Because you were there."

He nodded, but for once his expression was serious. There was no crinkling smile around the eyes. Instead, his eyes were dark and intense. "Good," he repeated. "So if I did this"—he pressed his lips to hers briefly—"I wouldn't be out of order?"

She took a breath as he pulled away. She shook her head. "Definitely not."

"In that case..."

The gentle pressure of his lips caressing and teasing hers increased as she opened her mouth, and his tongue slid against her lips and slipped into her mouth, touching the tip of her tongue.

Everything seemed to be in slow motion. She was preternaturally aware of the clatter of the palm tree in the wind, the heavy scent of the honeysuckle, and the bewitching sensation of his tongue caressing hers, his body pressed close, rousing long-forgotten desires.

She moaned against his mouth, as his tongue played with hers.

Too soon, he pulled away and cupped her face in his hands. "I'd never imagined we'd be kissing outside your family home."

"Me neither." She giggled. "I feel like a teenager, sneaking a boyfriend into my room."

"Now there's a thought which won't leave me in a hurry. Fancy sneaking into my room?"

She shook her head and took a deep breath. "You mean the room you're sharing with Max?"

"I'm sharing?"

"Yep. Afraid so."

"Then how about yours?"

"And I'm sharing with Aimee."

"Then I guess any more kisses will have to wait."

"Um," she murmured, wriggling closer to him. "Maybe one more to keep me going."

And he took her in his arms and made sure the kiss would keep her going for some time to come.

The next morning, Lizzi slept in and awoke after Aimee and the others had left the house for the beach.

Lizzi opened the windows and heard them and other voices coming from the beach. Looked like the tide was in and it sounded, from the splashing and shouts, that people were swimming already. Although Lizzi knew Aimee wouldn't be swimming as she was afraid of the water. She decided to go and join Aimee watching the others from the beach.

Lizzi emerged onto the seaward terrace, plucked a

flower and sniffed its fragrance. The green foliage overhead filtered the sunlight over the lawn, creating pools of flickering light which danced in the breeze. She'd forgotten how beautiful this place was.

She looked out from under the trees, across the beach. Amber was kicking a ball with Gabe, while Pete was swimming through the waves which were choppy, stirred by the brisk sea breeze. Max and Rachel were with Aimee, who was dressed in swimming shorts and a top, watching Pete swim. Rachel and Aimee were edging into the water when the football splashed Rachel, and she let go of Aimee's hand and went running after Gabe to get her own back. At the same time, Max dove into the sea and swam out to Pete.

Meanwhile, Aimee splashed in the shallows, jumping over the white-topped waves. Aimee knew the drill—keep to the shallows. Lizzi watched her siblings chase each other with a wet ball and laughed before glancing at Aimee. Aimee had called out to Pete and Max who hadn't heard. She edged a little further in.

There was another shout from Amber as Rachel splashed her and Lizzi looked toward them again. She turned to Aimee and couldn't see her. She appeared from behind the jetty. Lizzi frowned. She was getting in deeper than usual.

Lizzi felt compelled to go to her. All her protective instincts were screaming for her to go and look after her daughter but the voice of her father accusing her of being over-protective echoed in her mind. She willed herself to walk slowly to Aimee but quickened her pace as she noticed the waves were breaking over Aimee's shoulders, but still Aimee kept on moving forward. Surely either Max or Pete would look around and see her at any moment?

And still, Aimee moved forward, calling out to Pete and

Max, her small voice lost on the wind. Lizzi started to run toward the sea. There was no one nearer than Lizzi anymore.

Lizzi looked toward Aimee just as a wave splashed over her head. Aimee stumbled but stayed upright. Then another wave came, and another, and Aimee was submerged, her face appearing only briefly, its expression terrified as she gasped for air.

Lizzi shouted Aimee's name as she sprinted toward the place she'd last seen her. She called again, but her voice was carried to the house on the wind, away from the others on the beach who were laughing at Amber who was shaking her wet hair like a dog.

Then she saw Pete glance over his shoulder. He couldn't have heard, but something had alerted him and Lizzi shouted, and Pete turned further to see Aimee who, at that moment, surfaced briefly, spluttering before going under once more. Pete shouted something to Max, and they both swam toward where Aimee had last been seen.

Time slowed. Lizzi's legs didn't seem to work properly, and Pete disappeared, leaving nothing except a turbulent surface and another wave breaking. Lizzi opened her mouth to scream, the fresh salt air tearing at her lungs as she reached the shallows and then... Pete surfaced, pulling Aimee out of the water, wriggling and spluttering. Aimee clung to Pete as he came toward Lizzi, Aimee's face a vision of terror. Lizzi held out her arms and Aimee leaped into them, gasping.

They were met by her sisters and brothers holding out a big towel which she wrapped around Aimee. She coughed and was sick on the sand.

Lizzi wrapped another towel around Aimee who sat, shivering with shock, against her. Slowly Lizzi became aware of her siblings talking, wondering how it had happened and saw Max pacing the sand a short distance away, obviously blaming himself for not having been aware that Aimee was by herself.

Their gaze met and she shook her head, trying to reassure him, but he simply looked out to sea. She suddenly remembered how his best friend had died when they'd gone sailing together. Aimee's accident must have brought back bad memories. He'd always blamed himself.

She looked around to see Rachel, distraught, also blaming herself for getting distracted. She'd reassure them later. But now Aimee needed her undivided attention.

"Hush, Aimee, it's okay." Lizzi knew that Aimee's imagination and penchant for drama would blow the incident up sky high if she let it. "It happens to us all... a big wave comes and knocks us over. That's why I want you to learn to swim."

"But..." Aimee's teeth chattered as she lifted her pale wet face to Lizzi's. "I hate the water."

"Then why did you go in?"

"Because I wanted to join in. I wanted to be like the other kids at school."

Lizzi exchanged looks with Rachel before picking Aimee up and continuing along the path toward the house.

"Aimee?" They all turned around to see Pete looking at Aimee, his hand outstretched. "You need to learn how to swim."

Still shivering, Aimee looked up at Pete and Lizzi recognized the determined jut of her jaw. Aimee wriggled from her mother's grip and stood on the sand, pulling the towel around her.

Lizzi's heart gripped with fear. Shades of Charles all over again. "No! She's had a shock. She needs—"

"She needs to learn how to swim," he said firmly. He looked at Aimee. "Come on, Aimee, I won't leave you. But you need to make sure that doesn't happen again. Right?"

He looked directly at Lizzi. "Fear never leaves you unless you face it."

Lizzi looked at her daughter, wanting to hold her tight and never let her go. But she recognized Aimee's strong, determined gaze and backed off. She knew that expression because it was her own, and it had been her mother's. And once a decision had been made, there was no going back.

Pete squatted in front of the still trembling Aimee. "I'll teach you how to swim, Aimee."

"I can't! All the other kids say I'm useless."

Pete recovered quickly from the impact of the bullying words. "I promise you we'll show them that they're wrong. As soon as we get to Shelter Springs, we'll go to the swimming pool for lessons. After school. Okay?"

Aimee nodded, her lips still trembling but her eyes a little brighter with hope.

He rose. "Good. For now, you and I will go into the sea and have a bit of fun. Yeah?"

Lizzi and Max watched Pete and Aimee in the shallows. Aimee even managed to laugh when Pete fooled around in the waves with her.

"Kids get over things pretty quick, don't they?" said Max, narrowing his eyes against the sun.

"Superficially. I hate the fact that she hasn't told me about being bullied before."

"It was good of Pete to offer to teach Aimee to swim."

"Yes."

"He's fond of her."

"Um."

"And you."

She glanced at Max, but he was still focusing on Pete and Aimee.

"Maybe."

"Question is, what are you going to do about it?" He raised an eyebrow in query before going to join Amber and the others.

Lizzi stayed where she was, continuing to look out to sea, trying to figure out the answer to Max's question. Was it time to let the past events that haunted her slip away? But, more to the point, *could* she?

———

Pete and Lizzi arrived at The Lakehouse Café later that same evening. Pete had a late meeting at his house with the previous owner of the vineyard and Lizzi had paperwork to catch up on at the café.

Aimee had wanted to stay another night at Belendroit and return with Amber, who had agreed to stay for a few months to see Lizzi over the busy period. And, as they drew up to the café, Lizzi was very aware that, for the first time in a long time, she was alone with Pete.

Her staff had closed up the café some hours before, but Lizzi wanted to check it out before going to her cottage next door. The light was fading from the sky, and Lizzi switched on the lights and turned to find Pete closer than she'd imagined. And, from the look on his face, he wasn't thinking about the café.

"Thanks for inviting me to Akaroa. I enjoyed it."

"You're welcome. My family all think you're wonderful and..."

"You?"

She cocked her head to one side. "You're okay." She grinned.

"Lizzi," he said in a low, threatening voice.

She grinned. "More than okay. I enjoyed you being there, too. It made a big difference."

"Because I deflected attention away from you?"

She shook her head. "That, and..." She began to walk away, but he reached out and grabbed her hand and stopped her, forcing her to look at him.

"And?"

"And because I enjoyed your company."

He stepped closer, his lips quirked into a warm, seductive smile, and his eyes simply devouring her. "Anything else?"

She couldn't resist. She lifted her hand and ran her finger over his lips. He moved his mouth trying to catch her finger but she was too quick. "And the kiss. I *really* enjoyed the kiss."

She stepped back until their joined hands were outstretched, then let her hand fall. He didn't try to hold onto her. "You know, there are more kisses where that one came from." His eyes were indecent. "A lot more."

"I was hoping you'd say that. Want to come over later?"

"Hm, I'll have to check my schedule," he teased.

She shrugged. "I don't want to force you, but I thought it might be nice."

"Yeah." He grinned. "I think it will. How about I don't leave at all?"

She laughed. "You go. You'll miss your meeting. And I've got to cash up here and check emails and stuff. Come round to the house in a couple of hours."

"Only on one condition."

"And that is?"

"That you give me a goodbye kiss."

She put her arms around his neck and kissed him in a way which showed exactly how much she wanted him to return. She pulled away breathless, filled with desire and a light bubbling happiness she hadn't felt in years.

"And, if you want me to arrive any sooner, you know where I am." He indicated his house at the other end of the sweep of the lakeside bay. "In my house. We don't even need a phone. We can always communicate through code. Two flashes of the lights to say everything is all right. Three to say you want me. How about that?"

"And one flash? What will that be for?"

"It'll probably mean a bulb is gone. I'll bring you round a replacement."

She laughed.

"Right." He pulled away and walked toward the door.

"Have I frightened you off?"

"No, the sooner I get the meeting over and done with, the sooner I can return."

She laughed as she watched him walk across the dimly lit room, pick up his phone and keys and leave the café with one last wave.

She bolted the door behind him and, smiling to herself, went into the office. Then she heard someone walking up the steps and try the front door to the café. With the lights on inside, she couldn't see who it was, but knew it had to be Pete. She unbolted the door and smiled broadly.

"What have you forgotten?" she asked as she flung the door open wide to find Charles, her ex-husband standing there, perfectly groomed as always—the short hair, waft of aftershave and ironed clothes and polished shoes—and his ice-blue eyes, perfectly chilling as always.

"Forgotten, Elizabeth? Nothing. I've forgotten nothing."

Icy fear slashed deep inside her as, by sheer strength of personality, he forced her to stand to one side so he could walk into her café. He looked around, his intense eyes missing nothing. He raised his eyes to hers. "But I saw you from outside, I saw you kissing someone, and you ask what *I've* forgotten? You don't remember how much I hated the thought of you with another man?"

Fear robbed her of any thought. She shook her head, trying it to rid it of the dreaded apparition before her.

"You might not, Elizabeth, but I do. I remember everything."

CHAPTER SEVEN

Lizzi searched the dark street, hoping that Pete might still be around, but there was no sign of his car. No sign of anyone. No passers-by, no houses within shouting distance. Nothing but the silence of the night.

"Close the door, Elizabeth. It's cold out there."

She gripped the door, took one last look around and closed it behind her. She turned to face him. His large frame was lighter since he'd left the military, but he was still handsome, still imposing, and still gut-wrenchingly chilling.

He stepped toward her, and she flinched. A flicker of a smile passed over his lips—he'd always liked to see her afraid—but his hand only brushed her shoulder as it reached behind her and touched the framed photograph of the three of them—Charles, Lizzi and Aimee. Lizzi thanked God Aimee wasn't there. He picked up the photograph and looked at it. And then at her.

"The happy family," he said, his voice heavy with sarcasm. He replaced the photo. "I'm surprised you still have it on show."

"I did it for your mother's sake, when she used to come

into the café. And for Aimee's." She lifted her chin. She couldn't afford to look afraid—no matter how she felt. "Certainly not for mine. I can't be more pleased that you're out of my life."

"So it would seem. And the feeling's mutual. Except"—he brushed her cheek, and she couldn't prevent a startled gasp—"except for some reason I still don't like to think of you with anyone else."

She was suddenly afraid for Pete. She knew what Charles was capable of. "Not that it's any of your business, but I'm not with anyone else."

"You kiss all your friends like that?"

She shook her head. "That was... just a kiss. As you can see, he didn't stay."

"Yes, I noticed. Good." He considered her for a few moments and then walked around the café. "Thanks for agreeing to buy me out, by the way." He flashed her a false smile. "Makes things simpler." He frowned as he picked up an ornament and inspected it. "Mother's?" he asked.

She nodded. "Your mother liked the café, she was always bringing bits and pieces for it."

He grunted. "No idea why." He looked around. "It's a mess. At least it's not *my* mess anymore."

She gritted her teeth. "Charles, why are you here?"

"To sort out the estate."

"I thought that was all taken care of by the lawyer."

He shrugged. "Mostly. The property is going on the market shortly. I'm here to see if there's anything I want to take with me."

"I'm sorry about your mother, by the way."

"Yes, well, she was ill for a long time."

"It doesn't make it any easier, though. She was a wonderful woman."

He narrowed his eyes. "I suppose."

She glanced out the window. Still no sign of Pete. Nor of *any* car, she realized. "Where's your car?"

He sat. "I didn't hire one. I got a taxi here. There are cars at the estate, and I thought you could take me there."

The thought of being alone, in the middle of nowhere, at Charles's family estate, chilled her. "I can't do that, Charles. You'll have to get someone else to take you."

"Like who?"

"Ring for a taxi."

"I dismissed the only taxi around when I saw you. No. You can take me. Failing that, I'll stay here with you and Aimee tonight."

She shook her head. "No. There's no way you can do that."

"Why not?"

"Because I don't want you to. You're married to someone else, not to me. You have no right."

His brow lowered and his eyes hardened. Lizzi felt sick. "I have every right. You're the mother of my child. This place is still part mine—for a few more days at least. And you've said yourself that you've no man. What's wrong with one last night together? Hey?" His brow lifted and he came to her and swept a lock of hair from her cheek and tilted up her chin. He was much taller and his large hand held her face too firmly. He had to be aware of how much she shook. "You do remember, Elizabeth, how good we were together? How we used to make love all night? I remember exactly how you liked it... how to make you moan with pleasure... and the rest."

With his other hand, he began to push up her skirt, his fingers grazing the top of her thigh. Her terrified inertia suddenly left her and she slapped his hand away and tugged herself free from his grip. "Stay away from me." She looked around for her phone, but he followed her gaze and grinning, slipped it into his pocket.

"You don't need that."

She stumbled to the light switch and flashed it three times.

Pete had never felt less interested in wines. As the previous owner introduced him to an important exporter who expounded at great length on the minutiae of export—freight costs, landing prices and distribution channels—Pete's mind wandered to Lizzi, waiting for him at the café. The way she'd looked at him after they'd kissed—her full lips partly open, her eyes seductive and inviting, and her hair, falling around her shoulders—made him groan with arousal. The others looked up questioningly. He made some excuse, and the meeting continued.

Thankfully the meeting was brief as the exporter had a plane to catch and, after a memorandum of agreement had been signed, Pete was left alone. He briefly checked his emails, and, as he scanned a document, he looked up at the café across the lake.

The café was in darkness. And so was her house. Then the light went back on in the café. And then it went off. What on earth? He tried her cell phone while he watched three more flicks of the switch. There was no reply.

Lizzi switched the light on. What was keeping Pete? Surely he'd noticed her signal by now? She glanced over at Charles.

"What are you doing with the lights?"

She swallowed nervously. "The bulb's been flickering. I'm testing them."

"Well, don't!" he snapped. "It's giving me a headache."

Lizzi racked her brains, trying to remember how she'd coped with his mood swings. "Would you like a drink?"

"Whiskey."

"No!" There was no way he was having a whiskey—it had always been a prelude to violence.

"What do you mean 'no'?"

"I mean, we've run out."

"Run out?"

"We're a café. How about a hot drink? Hot milk, just as you used to like it?"

"I know you run evening functions, Elizabeth. Functions with alcohol. I've seen the books."

"But—"

He sighed. "I guess I *am* thirsty after the flight. Milk will be fine." He walked over to a table and sat.

She took the opportunity to disappear into the kitchen to fix him his favorite drink—hot milk. A child's drink, she'd always thought. Apt for a man who, for all his strength and courage, could act so childlike at times.

As she warmed the milk, she watched him surreptitiously. His presence dominated the café. He didn't sit in one of the easy chairs but on an antique spindle-backed chair, his fingers interlaced, his body perfectly still, as he looked around the café with a restless gaze. Perfect control, but watching all the time.

The sort of person who was capable of anything, she thought with a shiver. But hadn't he always been? It had been what had earned him the medal for bravery and what had made him impossible to live with.

She took the drink over to him, and she was relieved to

see her phone on the table in front of him. He downed the drink in one and placed it on the table next to her phone, and looked up at her in such a way as to make her take a step back.

She had to divert him, as she would a child. Maybe then she could keep him calm and retrieve her phone. "How are things in Indonesia? How's Maria?"

He frowned. "Fine. Life is good there. Maria suits me."

She nodded and smiled encouragingly. "I'm pleased for you. When we spoke on the phone, she seemed nice." Not only nice, Lizzi thought. But sensible—a no-nonsense type who, with her live-in extended family, was more than capable of looking after both Charles and herself. She racked her brain trying to think of something else to keep his temper under control. "Aimee's doing well."

"Aimee?" He nodded, as if he'd forgotten all about his daughter. "Good." He looked around. "Is she here?"

"No. She's with my family, in Akaroa." And for that, Lizzi thanked God. There was no way she wanted Aimee around Charles.

"Good," he repeated.

And, it seemed, that nothing had changed there either. Charles still didn't want to see Aimee.

"So... how long are you here for?"

He rose and came toward her, his head jutting forward belligerently. "What's with all the questions?"

"It's a polite inquiry, that's all."

"Is it? The answer is I'm here as long as it takes." He smiled. "Don't you like that idea, Elizabeth? I can drop in at any time."

"No, you can't. And if you try I'll take steps to stop you."

His gaze narrowed. "Are you threatening me?"

"No. I'm telling you."

A slow smile spread across his face which made it more chilling than before. "Just take me home, and we can talk another day. I'm tired now."

"Okay." She didn't want to, but there was no other way. She'd take him there, make sure she didn't get out the car, and then leave.

"It'll be like old times."

He made a sudden move toward her, and she backed up against the door, losing her balance. He grinned and grabbed the keys she'd tossed onto the table earlier. Suddenly the door swung open behind her revealing Pete, eyes blazing. He reached out and steadied her. Never in her life had she been so happy to see someone.

"Who the hell are you?" asked Charles.

"I'm Pete, Lizzi's friend."

Charles's eyes narrowed. "Lover?"

"No," said Pete. And for the first time, Lizzi was glad that they weren't. She didn't think Pete was capable of lying convincingly.

"Ah, but you're the guy who kissed my wife."

"Ex-wife, I believe."

"Whatever."

"I'm Pete, I've recently moved to the area. I'm also a friend of Max, Lizzi's brother. And you must be Charles. I recognize you from your photos." For all the anger she could see in his eyes, Pete was playing it cool.

"Ah," Charles said suspiciously. Pete extended his hand and Charles took it automatically.

Pete glanced at the car keys in Charles's hands. "Are you off out?"

"I'm taking Charles to his family's place," said Lizzi.

"That's not far from me, is it? Would you like a lift, Charles?"

Charles shrugged, taken by surprise.

"Why don't you turn in for the night, Lizzi, and I'll drive Charles? It'll give me a chance to try out my Dodge Challenger cross country. Have you taken a drive in one of the new SRT8s, Charles? It has a 6.4-liter V8 engine."

Pete took control of the situation, guiding Charles away from the personal to talk about cars as he opened the door for him to leave. And Charles responded—just as he would in the army—to someone calm and authoritative.

"Where are your bags?"

"On the porch."

Pete held the door open while Charles descended the steps to his bags. But Lizzi was concerned. What if Charles turned on Pete? Pete needed to know more about Charles—his triggers, and exactly what he was capable of—before he went off with him.

"Pete," Lizzi said quietly. "Can I have a few words?"

Charles jerked his head around. "Why?"

Pete surreptitiously tapped his pocket where his phone was. He was going to ring her later. He smiled reassuringly. She nodded. Besides, she could tell from the set of his face that nothing she could say would dissuade him from leaving with Charles. There was no way he was leaving Charles with Lizzi a moment longer.

Before anyone could change their minds, Pete followed a strangely docile Charles down the steps toward the waiting car. Without risking a further exchange of words, Lizzi watched Pete drive off with Charles and hoped that Pete would be all right.

.   .   .

While they spoke of the army—where they'd served and mutual acquaintances—Pete remembered everything Lizzi had alluded to about Charles. He felt sick to the pit of his stomach that this man had been able to hurt her. Even now, in the café, he'd seen the fear in her eyes when she'd looked at Charles. Pete flexed his hands around the steering wheel, as he continued to control the car over the rough inland road while, at the same time, control Charles's mood through the conversation, and not least, control himself.

At last, they arrived at the isolated house. As Charles called out his thanks and scrunched across the gravel drive toward the front door, Pete's mind returned to Aimee. Charles hadn't spoken of Aimee at all during the twenty-minute drive to his family home. Pete's heart ached for the little girl, and he thought of her fear of swimming.

How much easier it would be to help Aimee face her fears, than it would be to help Lizzi face hers. But then he glanced at the man disappearing into the dark house. Easy had never particularly appealed to him.

CHAPTER EIGHT

A nother week over. It had been two weeks since Charles had arrived and, thankfully—and inexplicably—Lizzi hadn't heard from him. She'd just wished she'd known in advance that he wouldn't contact her. Because every day had been spent looking over her shoulder, jumping at the sound of the doorbell, on edge, wondering if he'd show up.

Not that she'd had much time to worry. She'd been busy juggling phone calls, internet inquiries, marketing and financial plans, managing staff, working the front of the house, and everything else that went into managing a café.

It was the height of the tourist season, and the café was full to overflowing. She'd had to hire more tables and chairs which spilled out from the veranda and into the garden which led to the lake. But while she carried on as normal, every minute of every day she carried with her a fear that Charles would show up.

She might not have seen Charles, but she knew what he'd been doing, thanks to his estate manager who'd been a loyal friend to Charles's mother. Apparently, Charles had insisted on a thorough inspection of the large country station on horseback, as well as the contents of the house and financial paperwork. Charles was nothing if not thorough. And, for once, Lizzi was relieved. At least it meant that she and Aimee had been left in peace.

Lizzi took a sip of wine and put her feet up. The café was locked, and she could relax.

The door handle rattled, and she jumped up, spilling her wine. She peeped through the window. It was Pete.

She heaved a sigh of relief and opened the door.

"Hey, you!" He glanced at the spilled wine. "Hope that's not *my* wine you spilled." He grinned.

She walked over and poured him a glass. "I've been on edge all week, thinking it's Charles. As time passes, I can't help thinking the likelihood of him turning up increases."

"Only one more week and then he'll be gone."

"I can't wait." He sat opposite her. They'd agreed to keep their distance from each other while Charles was close by. But she wasn't sure sitting opposite her was the safest option, not with the way his gaze settled on her.

"Me neither." He took a sip of his wine. "Not least because he's keeping me from you."

"I want to be with you, too. I just can't risk him seeing us together. You don't know what he's like... what he's capable of."

"I know. But we could always go away."

"I can't." She waved a hand toward the café. "I've got too much on."

"You've got Amber. You've said she's brilliant—charming everyone front of the house."

"Yeah, she's been great. Not so good at the paperwork, though."

"That can wait. Max tells me you've refused his invitation to the summer party tomorrow night at his Queenstown Lodge."

"Of course I have. I don't have the time to make the three-hour trip to Queenstown, chat with the rich and famous, and then make the return journey. I'd miss out on two days' work."

"And only you would see that as a disadvantage! Seriously, though. You've described why you *should* go. Because the 'rich and famous' will be there. Max has an instinct for networking which you need to take advantage of."

Lizzi swirled the wine around in her glass. "I see your point. But, I don't know, it doesn't feel right to leave the café. I've got to make the first payment at the end of the month, and the bulk of it is going to come from next week's wedding."

"Ah, the big event."

"Indeed. Two days, one marriage and reception, and the loan repaid for one month."

"Right. And you're leaving everything until the last minute?"

"Of course not!"

"So... you've got everything prepared ahead of time."

"Everything. Absolutely everything. You know me. I'm not leaving *anything* to chance."

"Then you can come. You need to focus on next year and the year after that. Think of Queenstown as seeding time. You have enough staff to run the café. Amber won't mind taking over. She'll probably enjoy having the place to herself."

He leaned forward, and she had no choice but look into his seductive gaze. "You know I'm right. You can't afford *not* to go."

"Maybe. But..."

"But what?"

"I haven't anything to wear."

"*That* is the lamest excuse I've heard. Although, from what I've seen of your wardrobe, I can imagine it's a valid one!"

She threw the cork at him but, annoyingly, he caught it.

"Anyhow, we'll solve it by shopping in Queenstown."

"Okay. But I'm not leaving Aimee here. Not with Charles close by."

"Of course not. She'll come. Max has it covered. You won't be the only person with a child. He has a separate party organized for them. If you'd returned his calls, you'd have known."

"I was going to, but I was too busy today."

"So it's a deal?"

She grinned. "We can leave as soon as Aimee's swim sports are finished. She's going to be over the moon."

Pete grinned. "And I'll make sure you will be, too."

Lizzie thought she was more anxious than Aimee as she sat by the pool, watching the summer swim school's annual competition. She glanced at Pete who was sitting beside her. He betrayed no concern which was just as well, the number of times Aimee had looked up to him for reassurance.

Aimee's class was up next, and Aimee and the other kids were called to the pool. Lizzi saw a flash of nerves pass over Aimee's face.

Aimee looked up at Pete and Pete nodded reassuringly. Aimee's mouth tightened into a determined straight line as she followed the others down the steps and took her place at the end of the pool. Lizzi looked at Pete who, with only a simple smile, managed to convey to Lizzi that she wasn't to worry.

Then the gun went off, and Lizzi jumped, but Aimee's focus was total, and she was the first to push herself off the side onto her back and kick for all she was worth.

Lizzi gasped. She hadn't known Aimee had gained the courage to swim without floats. She really had come on since doing the lessons with Pete. While her kicking might lack finesse it seemed to be having the required effect, and she was a head in front of her closest competitor.

"Aimee!" Lizzi joined the cheers and shouts as Aimee and the others churned the water as they progressed up the pool. Aimee stared up at the pool's ceiling, waiting to see the flags overhead which signaled the end of the pool. Her expression astounded Lizzi. She'd never seen such a look of confident focus on her daughter before. She glanced again at Pete who was sitting forward, as focused as Aimee. He knew. He'd seen this growth in Aimee, but Lizzi hadn't. She suddenly realized why Aimee hadn't wanted her at swimming practice. At the time she'd been hurt, but now she realized that Aimee had wanted to show her how far she'd come at today's event.

People were jumping up and down, and Lizzi's voice was hoarse with shouting. The excitement reached its pitch as Aimee and another girl approached the finish. With two, long, strong strokes Aimee's hand touched the edge a second ahead of the other person. Aimee looked up to see a teacher raise a flag above her head. She'd won!

Lizzi made her way to the poolside and Aimee jumped out and gave her a big wet hug. Lizzi pushed away wet strands of hair. "Aimee! That was fantastic!"

"I won, Mum, I won!" She looked around. "Where's Pete?"

"Here!" he shouted above the noise. She turned around and he gave her a big hug.

Then Aimee was called away to sit with her class and Pete and Lizzi were left alone. "Pete, thank you so much, for what you've done for Aimee. I can't believe how much she's improved."

"All she had to do was realize how good she could be. And then her stubborn streak kicked in. She's pretty determined once she's made her mind up."

"You've given her so much confidence. I only wish I could have done the same."

"No problem. Anyway, I'm off."

"You're leaving?"

"No, I'm going to get changed. Aimee said there's a race for dads or uncles—don't think the organizers were too worried about actual titles—so I said I'd do it."

"That's good of you."

"No, it's not. I'm doing it to show off!" He grinned and she watched him disappear into the changing rooms.

He wasn't doing it to show off, and she knew it. He was doing it to be kind to her daughter. He was doing it to help her feel she belonged.

Lost among the crowd of families who sat on the wooden slats of the concrete terraces around the pool, she could give her full attention to Pete, as he walked up to the pool's edge wearing only swim shorts. Tall, lithe, with taut muscles that revealed him to be more of an athlete than many of the other dads, all Lizzi wanted to do was to go to him and run her hands over his broad shoulders, chest, and muscled stomach and—

Her thoughts came to an abrupt halt when the gun went off, and Pete dove smoothly into the water, not surfacing until half-way along the pool, after which he leisurely swam the length, before turning and racing the rest of the way. There had never been any doubt in Lizzi's mind that Pete would win the contest. And he did. With ease. He pushed himself out of the pool and did a high-five with Aimee as he walked across to his towel. Lizzi watched Pete towel dry his hair and thought about the weekend ahead. Somehow she felt it was going to be a good one.

On their way to Queenstown, they stopped off at Pete's vineyard and Lizzi and Aimee were given a personal tour. Lizzi had been there before and was impressed with the changes he'd achieved in such a short time. The high altitude of the vineyard and the cold winters produced unique flavors which had been selling well before Pete had purchased the winery but, with his flair for marketing, the wines were about to take off internationally.

Back in the car again, Aimee didn't stop talking or singing the whole trip. The relief of leaving the ever-present threat of Charles also made Lizzi light-hearted, and she joined in the singing. It felt a long time since the weekend away in Akaroa, even though it was only a month earlier.

The narrow road wound up the mountain pass and over into Queenstown—party capital of the lakes district. Before making their way up to Max's lodge, they stopped off in the town itself for a quick shopping expedition.

They walked along Queenstown's Beach Road with Aimee in between them, her hands tightly holding on to both of theirs. The day was bright and sunny. The mountain range which framed the lake, aptly called The Remarkables, was snow-capped and brilliant against the bright blue sky. And Lizzi felt happier than she'd been in a long time.

Her café was doing well, on target for repayments,

Charles would be gone in a week, and she had her favorite people with her. She glanced across at Pete who was answering one of Aimee's incessant questions with his usual patience and wit, and she felt a flood of love fill her, totally. She gasped and stopped walking. Aimee and Pete stopped and looked at her.

"Are you okay?" said Pete, concerned.

Lizzi didn't trust herself to speak. Her heart was too full. Instead, she nodded and re-gripped Aimee's hand.

"I think your mum needs some retail therapy, don't you, Aimee?"

"What's that?"

"Some pretty dresses bought for her!"

"Mum doesn't wear dresses."

"Then it's about time she did. And maybe you could do with a new dress, too?" Pete added.

Lizzi looked around the lakeside café with a professional eye. It was the second café they'd been in and, apart from a few details, what she saw confirmed that she was doing the right thing. Her café stood up well by comparison.

"The lighting's interesting, but I reckon the decor could do with a bit of personalizing."

She heard laughter and turned to see both Pete and Aimee grinning at her.

"What?"

"Mum," said Aimee leaning forward and grabbing Lizzi's hand. "You're taking a break, remember?"

She lifted Aimee's hand and kissed it. "Sorry, baby. Forgot myself for a minute."

Pete raised an eyebrow. "Only for a minute?"

"Of course!" She smoothed the dress she'd insisted on

buying herself. "How could I forget I'm on holiday when I'm wearing such a lovely dress?"

Lizzi stroked the fine linen-cotton mix, as smooth as silk, but by necessity, cooler for the heat of a high country summer. The white dress fitted her perfectly, molding to her slender curves before falling away to the mid-calf in a bias cut. The shoe-string straps and low neckline revealed the beginnings of a tan since she'd stopped covering up her arms so much. The scars on her arms were becoming less noticeable with each passing year, and she barely thought about them now. She felt like a million dollars. A far cry from the shorts-clad café owner, used to mopping up floors. She drew the line at high heels though. She reckoned twisting her ankle and falling over would probably ruin the look. Although she had relented on the issue of her hair. She'd let it fall loosely around her shoulders, instead of having it scraped off her face in her usual ponytail.

"You look really pretty, Mum."

"*Really* pretty," Pete repeated, with a heat in his eyes which made Lizzi blush.

She narrowed her eyes in warning as his gaze lowered to her breasts, but felt the pulse of desire deep inside. While Pete was busily devouring Lizzi with his eyes, Aimee was busily demolishing an ice-cream sundae, thankfully oblivious to the undercurrent of sexual tension. Lizzi grinned. She could get used to being a femme fatale.

It was a short ride up to Max's ski resort. With no skiing possible at that time of year, Max had transformed the resort into a summer getaway, complete with hot pools and swimming pool and an open-air marquee. The party was to celebrate the anniversary of his first year in operation. The car park outside the main stone building was filled with top-end Mercedes, BMWs, Ferraris and Lamborghinis.

"Glad I bought the Dodge, rather than the Land Rover," commented Pete wryly as he gave the key to the attendant to park. "Max definitely has a knack for gathering wealthy people around him."

"He has a knack for people. Full stop. Wealthy or otherwise."

"Looks like it's going to be an interesting party," said Pete as they caught a glimpse of a tall blonde stepping into a hot pool with a glass of Champagne.

Lizzi nudged him with her elbow. "Max isn't like that. Well, not now he's not. It'll be fun but entirely decent."

"Lizzi!" Max greeted them. "Great you could make it." He picked up Aimee and swung her around. "And how's my favorite niece?"

"I'm your *only* niece!" Aimee responded.

"Still my favorite," Max said, setting her to her feet. "Come with me, and I'll introduce you to the other kids."

Pete picked up a couple of glasses of Champagne and handed one to Lizzi, and they watched Aimee dash off with Max, firing questions as she went.

"I hope she'll get on with the others okay."

"Trust her. Leave her to it, and we can check on her later."

She smiled. "You're right. Of course, you're right."

"Now, let's go and mingle."

"Business or pleasure?"

"There's little difference in my book. My business is pleasure."

"So long as your pleasure isn't business," she added wryly as they walked across to a group of people.

. . .

Pete leaned back on the fence overlooking the ski fields that fell steeply away from the main building and looked over at Lizzi. Everything about her was bright, he thought. From her bright eyes, their rich brown glowing like molten choco-late, to her hair, its red streaks bright in the sunshine, to her white dress. He'd spent all afternoon with her but was enjoying himself even more now, simply watching her. She looked absolutely stunning. And it was clear that everyone else thought so, too.

"Enjoying the sights, Pete?"

Pete glanced around to find Max beside him.

"Sure am. You have a very beautiful sister."

Max laughed. "You're not even trying to hide the fact that you're ogling her."

"Nope!"

"She's been through a lot with Charles. I don't want her hurt."

"Is that a warning?"

"Yep."

"Well, you've no need to worry. I don't want her hurt either. And I won't because we both want the same thing."

"Lizzi's adamant she won't settle down again," Max warned.

"That suits me fine."

Max grunted. "Maybe. But I know I can trust you. I know she's in safe hands."

"She is," Pete said softly, his eyes never leaving Lizzi, who'd caught his eye and was making her way over to him.

Suddenly Max gave a long low whistle as a woman, dressed in ripped jeans and a tiny top, tore by on a moun-tain bike, blonde hair flying behind her, twisting and turning as she sped down a slope toward a jump.

Max followed her progress intently. Slowly, without

looking away from the woman, he placed his drink on the table and leaned over the balustrade of the restaurant's deck.

"Did you see her! Man, she can move."

Pete glanced at the woman and then at Max, whose eyes narrowed against the bright sunlight as he watched her take off from the jump and land in a cloud of dust. What she lacked in style and proficiency, she made up for in sheer guts.

Max laughed as she gave a great whoop, her infectious laughter filling the small valley as she jumped off her bike and went to join her friends.

"Max!" Lizzi grinned at him. "Is that the owner's perk— checking out sexy young women?"

"Who is she?" Max asked, ignoring her question. "An actress or model or something?"

"No idea. Whoever she is, she's popular. Looks like she's got quite a circle of admirers." Lizzi laughed. "Good luck with that one, bro!"

Rachel joined them. "That's Laura McKinney. She's the new YouTube sensation. She accepts dares and films them as she goes. She's quite something. Haven't you come across her? She's the darling of the media in the US. She's over here for a few weeks."

"In Queenstown? For a few weeks?" Max turned to Rachel. "How come I haven't heard of this?"

"An oversight of your PR manager, I'm sure," said Rachel.

"Hm," grunted Max. "Chelsey managed to get *you* here. That's a near miracle." He frowned, and Rachel looked away. "So," continued Max, "how come Chelsey didn't tell me about the famous Laura McKinney? She could be good for business."

"Laura doesn't do planning," said Rachel. "She arrives, she surprises, and then she's gone again. I doubt even Chelsey knew about Laura's intentions."

"Huh," grunted Max. "I pay her to know this kind of stuff."

"Why are you so annoyed?" asked Lizzi.

"Because that's the whole point of the summer party— to raise the Lodge's profile, to draw visitors to it—both summer and winter. That's why I have a PR team." He huffed an irritated sigh. "And, besides, I've made arrangements to leave for Australia in a couple of days."

"Ah, I get it," said Rachel. "Now you've seen Laura, you'd prefer to hang out here, rather than enjoy Sydney's high life. Although, seriously, Max, I don't think Laura is your type."

Max frowned. "And what's my type?"

Rachel and Lizzi exchanged knowing glances. "You know. Super-sophisticated, wealthy types. Jimmy Choo shoes, Birkin handbags, Ray-Ban sunglasses."

Max's frown deepened. "None of that means anything to me."

"No, but the type of women wearing them does."

"Give up, Rachel, he's a lost cause."

But Max seemed oblivious to their teasing and continued to watch the blonde below the terrace.

"You won't get anywhere there, Max, so I wouldn't even bother," said Rachel.

The idea of a woman turning him down was a new one to Max. "Why? Doesn't she like men?"

"Oh, she likes them all right. Likes them enough to insist that she'll never go out with anyone longer than a month. She's publicly stated that long-term relationships are for idiots and marriage is ridiculous."

"My kind of girl, then. See you later."

Lizzi and Rachel watched Max descend the steps and make a beeline toward the group at the center of which Laura held court.

"Do you think he has any idea what he's in for?" asked Lizzi.

Rachel shook her head. "Nope. A lamb to the slaughter."

Lizzi laughed. "It's sure going to make interesting viewing."

"And most of it on YouTube. Yep, he's going to need all the help he can get. Starting now." Rachel followed Max down the steps, leaving Pete alone with Lizzi.

"Having fun?" asked Pete as he went and stood beside Lizzi. He was pleased to note that when her shoulder bumped his arm, she didn't move away, but stayed close. He sighed and shifted his arm along the rail so that it was almost around her.

"Yes. You know those guys I was talking to earlier? Well, they think The Lakehouse Café would make a great base for some filming they're going to be doing in the Mackenzie high country. And I'm thinking that we could convert the building we're using for wedding receptions into a permanent function room."

"Great idea. If you want a backer for the finance, you know where to come."

"Thanks, but you know I want to do this on my own, without help from anyone else."

"Because of Charles?"

Sadness shadowed her eyes, and he regretted bringing Charles up. It was as if the sun had disappeared. She nodded. "Yeah. Can't seem to help it. Dad was both supportive and capable of knocking me down as I was growing up. It undermined my confidence. And then, Charles. I stayed too long with him." She glanced at Rachel enjoying herself with Max and the blonde woman who'd caught his attention, on the slopes below. "I need to go forward on my own." She paused and then looked up into his eyes. "Financially speaking, that is."

Despite the sense of unease that her words gave him, he couldn't help but respond to the twinkle in her eyes. "Just financially speaking. So"—he shrugged—"maybe some physical closeness wouldn't be uncalled for?"

"Um, I'm thinking, you could be right."

"Come here, Lizzi." He pulled her to him, slipped his arm around her shoulders and kissed the top of her head. "About time." He pressed his forehead to hers. "Your place or mine."

She pushed him away, laughing. "Neither! Yet..." She glanced across at where Aimee and the other children were playing some organized activity involving paint guns. "We can't slip away yet. Later, Pete. Later."

"Okay. Then I'd best not let you out of my sight until 'later' comes."

And he didn't.

Lizzi tiptoed into the room of sleeping children and pulled the cover over Aimee's shoulder and gave her a light kiss. Aimee didn't move.

Lizzi raised her eyebrows at Pete and walked quietly out and closed the door. "She's out for the count."

"I'm not surprised after what I saw earlier. Rachel had them running around playing some game which looked like a mix of hide and seek and bull rush."

"Bull rush?" asked Lizzi.

"Don't tell me you haven't heard of that game? It's pretty full on. I got concussed in a game at school once."

She lifted up her hand. "Enough! I don't want to know."

He laughed and put his arm around her, and they walked along the corridor to her room. They stopped in front of her door, and he turned her around in his arms.

"Here's your room, which Max so discreetly booked for you."

"And yours is?"

"Next door. Care to see it? I have a bottle of Champagne chilling, just in case..."

"In case I was curious to see your room?" She raised an eyebrow.

"Exactly." They walked to his door which he opened. "I thought, maybe Lizzi will be curious to see what more of the guest accommodation looks like."

She stepped inside. "Exactly like my room, as it happens."

"Well, then. With the tour over we can get down to business." He took her hand and pulled her to him and kissed her briefly, his lips sweeping hers. He pulled away and her mouth followed his, wanting more. Instead of continuing the kiss he smiled, a very confident, sexy smile, and walked over to the table in front of the open French windows and opened the Champagne, the cork bouncing off the wall.

"You're teasing me," she said quietly, trailing her hand across his back before stepping outside onto the veranda. "Two can play at that game."

He followed her outside and handed her a glass of Champagne. The bubbles popped and sparkled in the starlight, echoing the fizz of excitement inside her. She took a sip and leaned over the rail, looking out at the lights of Queenstown far below. "Mum's family used to own the resort, you know—years ago. It was a wreck when Max took it on. Now look at it. And look at that view, it's fantastic."

"And fantastic in a different way in winter, I should imagine. Snow everywhere."

"His business is going to do well."

He tapped his glass against hers. "Forget business for once. Here's to you and me."

She watched him as she sipped her Champagne. They hadn't switched on any lamps inside the room. The only light fell from the vivid stars which filled the dark indigo sky. One side of his face was shaded and, on the other side, only the planes of his cheekbones and nose and jaw were illuminated. And his eyes, icy white in the light.

Still, she hesitated. She was fighting against years of caution and intention. Should she break it all with this one moment? She answered it for herself as she brought her hand up to his face and cupped his cheek, stood on tiptoe and kissed him.

She gasped under his mouth, waiting to see what he'd do next. Wanting him to do a million things at the same time. He did nothing except whisper one word against her lips. "Lizzi..." She felt his breath in her mouth, and all she could think about was wanting more.

She swept her lips against his, breathing him in, feeling the warmth of his body against hers. His fingers caressed her neck and the kiss deepened, his tongue touching hers and sending her to a whole new level of passion. All her senses were contained in her mouth. She could think of nothing else but her needs. Her body melted into his as his hands moved from her neck, sweeping around her back before cupping her bottom and pulling her to him. She moaned and shifted against his hard form, heightening her pleasure... and his.

She pulled away, suddenly aware of what she was about to do.

"Lizzi, I want you. More than anything. Come to bed."

She shook her head and leaned her forehead against his. "And I want you, Pete. But it's been so long since I trusted anyone and I'm scared."

He inhaled a deep, ragged breath. He swallowed and then pulled away, his hands still around her. "Okay. Let's take things slowly. I'll prove to you that I can be trusted little by little." He tilted her chin up so she could look in the eyes. "Okay?"

She nodded.

"Besides, slow is good," he said, the sexiest look spreading over his face. And she suddenly wasn't so sure that "slow" was what she wanted.

CHAPTER NINE

This time when his lips found hers, it was with a soft, seductive caress that halted her crazy rampaging need for his body, changing it to a highly intense sense of anticipation.

She was acutely aware of every subtle shift of his lips as they brushed and teased hers. Her mouth was like a magnet, not wanting his to leave hers, as he kissed each side of her mouth. She was only aware of his breath on her face and of the collapse of her world into one moment, one action—this kiss.

Then he cupped her cheeks, and pulled away and the hot, wondering expression in his misty eyes made the breath catch in her throat.

"You're so beautiful..." he whispered, his voice husky with desire.

And, as he lowered his mouth to hers again, she believed him.

This time he traced his tongue between her partly closed lips, and she sighed as she opened them to allow him entrance. He slid his tongue inside and found hers and groaned as his hands moved over her shoulders, down to the small of her back, before coming to rest on her hips. She couldn't help herself—she tilted her hips toward him briefly before pulling away from the kiss, breathless.

He didn't make a move to draw her to him but looked at her with a slight frown. "You know I want you, Lizzi." She stepped away. "What—"

Whatever he was about to say was forgotten as her hands went to the side zip of her dress and slowly drew it down. She watched with satisfaction as he licked his lips. He didn't move. She wanted to *show* him how much she wanted him, and he understood. The thought of his total sensitivity to her thoughts, how in tune with her he was, gave her even more confidence to continue.

With the zipper undone, she slipped off first one strap, then the other and let them fall. But the neatly fitting bodice didn't move. He looked up and caught her gaze.

"Would you like a hand?"

She bit her lip and nodded. She had no experience of seducing a man. But it looked like this man didn't need to be seduced. He already was.

He stepped forward and pulled at the straps but he didn't force them beyond her breasts where the bodice stayed. He dipped his head and feathered kisses down her throat, her chest and the rapidly rising mounds of each of her breasts. And then he gave a sharp tug to her dress and she gasped as it fell down.

She suddenly felt awkward. "Pete, please." With her hands still on his shoulders, she urged him to lift his lips from her breasts.

But he was immovable. He took her hands and gripped them. "I'm not going anywhere. Yet." Then his mouth became too busy to talk.

And suddenly she didn't want him to go anywhere.

Much later, they lay, limbs tangled and bodies still connected in a bond both were reluctant to break, as their breathing slowly returned to normal. But when "normal" arrived, Lizzi knew that nothing would ever be normal again.

She lay looking up at the ceiling, blinking, trying to hold back the ridiculous tears but failing. A sob escaped her lips and Pete looked up at her, sweeping his thumbs against her cheek.

"Lizzi! What's the matter? Did I hurt you?"

She gulped in a shuddering breath and shook her head. "No. It's just, it's just..."

"Hush," he said, comforting her in the only way he could, with his hands, his voice, his kisses, his body. "Hush, it's okay."

"I..." But she couldn't tell him how she felt. She didn't have the words or control to explain what it felt like to have had the gates she'd kept closed for so long, guarding herself from hurt and feeling, demolished for good. She could hardly speak, let alone express how she'd been afraid she'd never get close to anyone ever again. But she had. And now she didn't think she'd ever get enough of Pete.

No, all she could do was show him how much he meant to her and how changed she felt. Show him... fingertip by fingertip, kiss by kiss, body against body.

And she did, throughout the night, while they talked and made love. Nothing as fast and furious as the first time, but slowly, sensuously. The pleasure they took in each other became more profound each time they made love, deepened by the different emotions their words and their bodies wrought.

The cool light of pre-dawn fingered its way into the un-curtained room, creating detail from the vague mounds of clothes strewn where they'd landed, from the swell and line of Lizzi's body.

She shifted in his arms, and he kissed the smooth skin of her shoulder. She moaned in that totally seductive way of hers, and then settled back into sleep. But not Pete. How could he? His eyes had been opened. He'd thought he was having fun in his life, keeping his relationships casual, moving on when he needed a change, but all the while he'd been running from love. And he didn't know it until now.

How could he have fooled himself that anything about his relationship with Lizzi could be casual? It was... *she* was... everything he hadn't dared to imagine. She'd made things clear to him—crystal clear—as clear as the cold, bright Mackenzie skies in winter.

Making love to Lizzi, her opening up to him in every way possible, had touched him to the depths of his soul, branded him, and he knew he would be hers forever.

He let his mind drift to their lovemaking and felt himself stir once more at the memory. And then he thought of her tears—and his own, which she hadn't seen. She'd tried to describe how she felt in the night, but she hadn't needed to.

He lifted his gaze to the sky where threads of orange and pink hung in the clouds above the mountains, deep-ening and changing as the sun filled the sky with its unseen rays.

She hadn't needed to because he understood perfectly—because he felt the same way.

A leisurely brunch on the terrace overlooking the grassy ski slope, framed by mountains, meant it wasn't until late morning by the time they got away.

Max and Lizzi followed Pete and Aimee to the car.

"Sorry we have to leave early, but Aimee has a birthday party. Her first sleep-over. She doesn't want to miss it."

"That's my niece. Takes after her Uncle Max. Never one to miss a party. Anyhow, you seem pretty smiley this morning. Had a good night?" asked Max with a raised eyebrow.

"Yes, thank you. Your beds are very comfortable."

"Hm, good." Max grinned. "About time."

Lizzi let it go. Max knew her, and she knew him. They didn't need to go into detail to understand what the other was going through. "And you look like the cat who had the cream. Although, no doubt, she'll be gone within a few weeks."

His grin morphed into a frown. "What do you mean?"

"You know exactly what I mean, Max Connelly. You make sure your relationships only last a few weeks. A few months, tops." They reached the car, and she turned to him. "It's almost as if you don't want to allow anyone close to you."

"Yeah, well, you'd know all about that."

"I do. And I think I've discovered that I've been wrong not to trust anyone before."

Max lifted his narrowed gaze to Pete who was collecting flowers with Aimee. "Pete?"

She nodded. "Pete." She wrung her hands as she tried to put into words what she felt. "He's different. I can trust him."

"Good." Max pulled Lizzi to him in a warm embrace. "I'm happy for you." He narrowed his eyes. "Just don't try to change *me*. I'm happy as I am."

She shrugged. "That's okay. You'll know when the time comes."

He shook his head and called over to Pete. "Take my sister away before she tries to change me any more."

Pete laughed and swept Aimee, complete with a huge bunch of wildflowers, into the car. He put his arm around Lizzi and she leaned into him, welcoming the sense of possessive affection for once. "Sure I'll take her away. But I can't promise she won't change you. Knowing Lizzi, it won't be from want of trying."

She shrugged. "I like to share the joy."

"You already are, darling," Pete said, and his eyes melted her all over again.

"You two! Go now, before I throw up!"

Pete laughed, kissed Lizzi, and they both got into the car.

Aimee waved all the way down the winding mountain road, not wanting to lose sight of her Uncle Max.

"Sit back, Aimee, your seatbelt's twisting."

"But I want to see Uncle Max!"

"Why? You've spent the morning hanging out with him."

"I wanted to see if he'd throw up. I wondered if it would look like my spew, you know all—"

"Aimee!" Lizzi spluttered.

. . .

Four hours later and Lizzi waved goodbye to Aimee who was immediately swallowed by a hoard of children at Glencoe. She got in the car with Pete.

"I hope she's okay."

Pete drove off. "Why wouldn't she be?"

"She doesn't often have sleepovers."

"Is she nervous?"

"No."

"Has she had bad experiences with sleepovers? Nightmares? Sleepwalking or something?"

"No."

"Are you worried about her not being looked after?"

"She's with Gemma and Callum—of course not!"

"Then stop worrying and focus on what we're going to do."

"What's that?"

"The café's closed?"

"Yes."

"No visitors expected?"

"Check."

"Then we have an afternoon, evening and night when I shall be your sex slave."

Lizzi laughed. "Sex slave?"

"Exactly. Whatever you want, darling. Whatever, however, *wherever*, you want." And he slid his hand up her leg.

Lizzi's laughter changed into a gasp.

The afternoon passed into evening, filled with lovemaking, wine and an ever-present flow of food from Lizzi's capacious fridge. Replete, they lay naked in the moonlight, looking across the lake while they talked and sipped wine. Only to fall into each other's arms once more and drift into sleep.

When Lizzi finally awoke, the sun had broken through the early morning mist which lay, wraithe-like, over the lake. She stretched out in his arms, relishing the feel of the fine cotton against her naked skin and the sense of a well-used body.

"Good morning, Lizzi." He kissed the top of her head. "About time you woke up. How do you feel?"

"Guess." She smiled.

"No. Tell me." His face was serious. "You don't regret what we did?"

She shook her head. "No, of course not. How could I? It was fun—"

"Fun? Was that all it was?"

She pressed her hand against his chest, splaying her fingers wide. "Don't interrupt. Listen to me. It was fun but more than that, it changed me."

He touched her cheek and then brushed his knuckles gently against her face. "How so?"

She angled her face toward his hand. "I can't get enough of your touch now." She sighed. "You opened me up. I felt like I'd been shut down for years, scared to allow myself to feel anything deep for anyone. Nothing that would make me vulnerable."

"I'll take good care of you, I promise." He smiled. "I won't let anything happen to you. You can trust me—you know you can."

"I know. I think I know, now."

Later that morning they parted—Lizzi to the café and Pete to return to the winery—then Lizzi spent the afternoon with Aimee, only returning to the café after it had closed, to finish up some paperwork.

It was only much later, after she'd put a very tired Aimee to bed, that her phone rang. She went outside onto the terrace and looked across the water to Pete's house. A lamp was lit, and a man's silhouette stood before it. She raised her hand in a wave, even though it was too far for him to see.

"I've just waved at you," she whispered into the phone.

"And I've just blown you a kiss."

"Thank you. I thought I felt a puff of air on my cheek."

He laughed, a low, sexy laugh which warmed her heart. "Wouldn't be anything to do with the breeze blowing across the lake?"

She shook her head. "No. Nothing whatsoever to do with the wind."

There was silence as his laughter died. "I miss you."

She smiled and looked away, trying to contain the surge of happiness which his words evoked. "Me too."

"What are you doing tomorrow?"

"Working. Monday morning. I've got the build up to the wedding."

"Ah, the wedding. I bet you're more excited about this wedding than your own."

It was her turn to be silent. "I no longer think of weddings as the be all and end all. It's what happens afterward that's important."

"I guess you're right. I've never been married, so can't comment."

She laughed. "You? Can't comment? Doesn't sound like you."

"Oh, I have my thoughts on marriage, of course I do."

"And what are they?"

"Are you free tomorrow night?"

She practically cradled the phone in her neck. "Yes," she whispered.

"Then I'll tell you then."

"Right..."

"Give Aimee a kiss from me."

"Will do. Do I get one?"

"I've already sent you yours. The puff of wind, remember?"

"That's all I get?"

"Until tomorrow," he whispered.

"Goodnight."

"Goodnight."

Lizzi tapped the phone and watched the shadow across the water walk back inside. *Tomorrow*, she repeated to herself. She could hardly wait.

It was the earthquake which awoke them. Lizzi opened her eyes wide and froze—all her senses instantly alert. Then it came. A sound like a thundering train, followed by a sharp jolt as the first wave hit.

She jumped out of bed and ran out the door toward Aimee's bedroom as Aimee cried out. Aimee's cries grew as the earthquake intensified, windows rattled, ornaments fell over and a crash came from the sitting room. Lizzi tried to run faster but, as the second rolling waves hit, she was thrown off-balance. She lurched from side to side, pushing herself from one wall to the other, as she made her way along the corridor toward Aimee's room.

By the time she burst into the room, the rolling was beginning to subside and the clattering of the windows in their frames was beginning to diminish.

"It's okay," she said sitting on the bed and pulling Aimee into her arms. "It's okay," she repeated as the house slowly stopped swaying and came to a halt. "It's okay," she repeated, as much trying to convince herself as Aimee. She kissed the top of her head and rocked her as if she were a baby again. "But you've got to learn to 'drop, cover and hold', Aimee. Don't they teach you that at school anymore?"

"Yes," Aimee gulped. "But I forgot because I was scared."

"Come on, let's go and get a drink and check things out."

She switched on the light and looked around. It had sounded and felt worse than it had been. Only a couple of things appeared to be broken. Some glasses and a vase— which she'd recently moved and hadn't got around to sticking on the shelf with Blu-Tack—had smashed on the floor.

"Lie over there, Aimee, pull the throw over you while I tidy up and get us a drink."

She picked up a few shards and rose and looked out toward Pete's house. There was a single light shining upstairs. Then her phone rang. She ran to the bedroom and answered it.

She sighed with deep relief as she walked to the window again and looked across the lake once more. His first thought must have been of her and Aimee. Their call lasted only long enough to reassure him that they were fine and that they'd meet up the next evening, after Pete had had a chance to check over the winery. They both had other calls to make—for Lizzi, to check her family were all okay in Akaroa, which much to her relief, they were.

With an earthquake, you never knew where its center was—whether you'd experienced the worst of it, or whether there were people elsewhere in the country whose houses had been destroyed and their loved ones killed. A quick check on the internet revealed that although earthquake was centered nearby and was of a relatively high magnitude, it was very deep and there was no major damage done.

After tucking Aimee in bed, Lizzi made a quick check on the café next door before returning to her house. She glanced at the clock; it was five in the morning. Hardly worth going back to sleep, even if she could. Instead, she lay on the couch, under a throw and looked out at the new day breaking across the lake. Before she knew it she was asleep.

But later that morning, Lizzi wasn't so relaxed. As soon as she switched on her computer, the cancelations began to arrive. News of the earthquake had spread quickly. Christchurch airport had been closed because of it. And it was to Christchurch that the overseas wedding parties would be coming, so they'd canceled. And Lizzi had nothing to show for all the work and orders she'd made for the imminent weddings.

She couldn't believe it. After everything had been running so smoothly, to receive these two cancelations which were crucial for her to make her monthly repayments, was unbelievable. But it was there in black and white. The figures didn't lie.

She picked up her printout of her revised spreadsheet and stared at the bottom line. Nowhere near enough to repay her bank loan. How was she going to replace her income? No one organized parties or weddings at a week's notice. Except, obviously, the people who'd canceled hers. She picked up the phone reluctantly. There was nothing for it. She'd have to go to the bank and ask for an extension based on some ideas she had for future events.

Lizzi sat nervously in the chair, waiting for the bank manager to reply to her brief explanation of events. He frowned a little as she spoke, read through her file and gave her a warm smile.

"That's fine, Mrs. Burnett. No problem there." He rose from his chair as if there was nothing more to be said.

It was her turn to frown. "No problem?" she replied faintly. She'd hoped that he'd be agreeable but hadn't expected him to be. "Don't you want to look at my revised budget for the next six months?"

The manager rose and held the door open with a smile. "No, I don't think so. Everything's fine."

"Fine?" she repeated faintly. How could there be 'no problem' and 'everything's fine', when it patently wasn't?

"Sir!" someone called out. "An urgent call for you."

"Sorry, Mrs. Burnett, I have to go now. But don't hesitate to get in contact if there's anything else I can help with."

Again Lizzi frowned, even as she nodded. His attitude had changed from deep suspicion the previous meeting, to wholehearted warm support. Why? *She* knew she was a sure bet—without earthquakes, that was—but she didn't kid herself that the bank looked any further than a spreadsheet.

"Sure, thanks." She followed him to the door as he took the phone from the receptionist. Still trying to figure out what was going on, she reached into her handbag for her keys only to find them missing. She glanced around and saw them still on the desk. She went and picked them up and noticed the manager's closed file on the desk.

She glanced at him. He had his back to her while he spoke on the phone. She quickly flicked the file open and twisted it around so she could see what notes, if any, he'd made about the meeting.

But there were no notes. Only a document she didn't recognize—some kind of memorandum. She flipped it over and saw a document she most definitely *did* recognize—her loan agreement. She flicked to the cover sheet. The memorandum was a loan guarantee. A wave of nausea came over her as she looked at the signatures at the bottom of the page.

She'd always teased Pete about his unrecognizable scrawl. But he was right. His name might not be legible, but it was immediately identifiable—that signature was definitely his.

A quick scan told her all she needed to know about why the manager had changed his attitude to her. She closed the file and straightened it on the desk, feeling sick to the pit of her stomach. She walked out into the bright sunshine without a backward glance.

Trust him, Pete had told her. Ha! That was a joke. How could she trust someone who'd gone behind her back? How could she trust someone who'd manipulated her, treated her like a child and gone to the bank, underwritten the loan, and then had the gall to return to her and celebrate her newfound 'independence'?

How could she trust someone who'd betrayed everything she was working toward?

CHAPTER TEN

She knew where Pete would be. Where he was twice a week these days—continuing to teach Aimee how to swim at the local pool. That, too, now felt like a breach of her trust in him. He'd got close to them, infiltrated the barrier she'd built to protect them both, through deceit.

The swimming pool was crowded and Lizzi only just managed to control the impulse to march over to him and give him a piece of her mind. But not while Aimee was here.

As she seated herself to one side, Pete looked up and smiled. He was in the pool, gently holding Aimee's shoulders as she lay on her back with a wide grin on her face, working on her kicking technique and splashing everyone in the process. Not even *that* was enough to reduce the anger and hurt that roiled inside her.

She glared at Pete and his expression changed to a puzzled frown as he focused once more on trying to refine Aimee's technique.

After five minutes Pete drew the lesson to an end and

Aimee climbed out the pool and over to Lizzi who handed over her bag. Aimee went into the changing room leaving Pete, looking like a god, standing dripping before her. Tall, tanned and muscled, with his golden hair wet from the pool, he looked like the answer to every woman's wildest daydream. Every woman, that is, except her.

He picked up his towel and slung it around his neck. "What's up, Lizzi? Something wrong?"

Damn him. Not only handsome, but caring, too. Somehow, it only made his deceit feel worse. She felt as if she'd been tricked. She hadn't seen what he was really like behind that perfect facade. *She*, who should have known about that old saying "appearances can be deceptive". *She*, who should have known better than to trust someone. Tears pricked behind her eyes. How *could* she have been so stupid?

"You *bet* there's something wrong. I went to the bank this afternoon to ask for some leeway on the loan repayment."

"Ah." He grimaced ruefully.

"Yes, *ah*! How dare you, Pete? How dare you go behind my back? You had no right to underwrite the loan. Do you think I'm some child, some *imbecile* who needs looking after?"

"No, of course not—"

"Well, it sure looks like it from where I'm standing. What makes you think you can step in, without being asked, and take over my life? It's what I've spent the past three years trying to get away from!"

"I was trying to help, and I knew you wouldn't want me to. But you needed the loan, and I could help you get it. Simple as that."

"Nothing, *nothing* is that simple, Pete. Least of all me. Least of all my situation." She looked around and lowered her voice. "You might not know everything about my past, but you knew enough to have understood why my independence was important to me."

"Look, Lizzi, when I guaranteed the loan, I wasn't aware of what had happened between you and Charles. What you suffered."

"Later you were, and you still didn't tell me."

He shrugged. "I didn't see the point."

"No point?" she exploded. "There might be only one point, but it's a darn good one. It would have been *truthful*, Pete. I wouldn't have had to stumble across what you'd done myself. I wouldn't be standing here wondering what else you haven't told me, what other reason there might be for me not to trust you!"

"There *are* no reasons! Yep, you're right. I shouldn't have done it without telling you. But, you know, I wanted to help. That's what I do when I care for people—my mother, my friends, my *sister*—I help them."

"Your sister?" Lizzi began to ask. He'd barely mentioned her before, and the emphasis he gave the word stopped her in her tracks.

"But seems like I was wrong. You don't want my help, just like my sister didn't." His voice had changed, become cold and measured, reminding her of the chill and control of Charles.

"I don't need anyone's help."

Anger blazed through her as they stood facing each other, oblivious to the curious stares sent their way. A muscle twitched in his jaw as he ground his teeth, words unspoken, feelings repressed. He backed away.

"Fine. And I don't want to be with a woman who doesn't trust me; I don't want to be with someone who doesn't believe in me, doesn't see me for who I am. And if I've described you, Lizzi, then let's finish this right now."

Lizzi opened her mouth to speak, but the words didn't emerge. She was hurt, she was angry, and she didn't know if she'd ever be able to trust Pete again, but she suddenly realized with appalling clarity that it was too late to stop herself from loving him. But that still didn't mean they had a future.

"So, do we finish this?" Pete asked.

"It's not that simple."

"Yes, it is."

She raked her fingers through her hair, holding her aching head. She'd never felt so confused. Her anger was slipping away from her, evaporating like steam into the cool air of reason, replaced by regret that she'd hurt him, and fear that she was about to lose him. "I don't know what to think."

"You would if you wanted a future with me. It's obvious you don't."

Suddenly Aimee came running through the door, tossing her bag to Lizzi.

"Mum! Did you see me? Pete says I'm getting really good!" She laughed and grabbed Pete's hand. "Didn't you, Pete?"

With his eyes never leaving Lizzi's face, Pete carefully disentangled himself from Aimee. "I've got to go now, kiddo."

"Oh." Aimee's face fell. "I thought you were taking me to the party."

"Change of plan. Your mum is."

"Oh, okay." Aimee went and pressed her nose to the

steamy window to look outside at some kids playing in the playground, leaving Lizzi and Pete alone once more.

"So?" Pete's question hung between them like a guillotine waiting to fall—the wrong answer would have it slamming down and severing everything that had grown between them.

Part of her wanted to tell him to go to hell. But part of her had just witnessed Aimee's obvious affection for him, emphasizing how he'd infiltrated their lives so thoroughly—like ivy on a damaged wall, invading the very mortar that held it together. Part of her felt she and her world might fall apart without him, which was the very thing she *didn't* want to feel. She had to either work out how she could extricate herself from him, or how she could stay with him. Neither path would be easy.

"We need to talk it through," said Lizzi. "Why don't you come over tomorrow evening? Let's meet in my office at the café." She couldn't trust herself to see him in her cottage. "Aimee's away at Glencoe."

"I'll see you there."

She held the door open for Aimee, and they both stepped out into the warmth of the late afternoon.

She listened as Aimee chatted about her friends at school, about swimming, and about Pete. *Pete.* She still felt the bitter sting of betrayal undermining all that they'd built over the past few months, but it seemed he'd only done what he'd done out of concern for her, and because that's what he'd always done. Stepped in, and been the Prince Charming. It might have worked out for him the past; it wouldn't work with her. Because her past told her that behind every Prince Charming there was a devil waiting to spring.

Pete swung the ax and the blade fell with an echoing thud, splitting the center of the wood and sending slivers of wood flying onto the pile that had accumulated over the past few hours. He immediately set another log in its place and swung the ax high, relishing the pain of his over-worked muscles as they slammed the ax down, splitting the log with a crack.

His panting breath drew in the scorching hot, dry air and the smell of resiny wood. He paused for a moment, wiping away the stinging sweat that trickled into his eyes with the back of his hand. He hadn't meant to stop because he knew what would happen if he did. And he'd been right.

He saw nothing of what was around him—not the beautiful home, the majestic mountains, the soaring golden grassy hills that went on forever, not the brilliant blue of the lake before him, and not least the café and its neighboring cottage which he'd spent so long contemplating over the past months.

No, now all he could see was the image of his sister's face, heart-shaped and as sweet as her spirit; and all he could think of was how he hadn't been able to protect her.

Alitia had traveled the world on a motorcycle, her only companion an unshakeable belief that everyone was fundamentally good. Every time he'd seen her—either on her rare visits home, or when he'd managed to track her down overseas—he'd tried to talk sense into her—tried to make her see what danger she was putting herself into. But she'd always laughed and refused to listen. And she'd paid the price.

He swung the ax again, the splitting of the wood piercing the evening stillness, but not healing his wounds.

And he never wanted them to heal. Because how could he forgive himself for not having seen how bad his influence on her had been? For not being there for Alitia, for not having insisted she return home to him, home to the safety of her family? She'd been too young to understand the world, and too headstrong to listen to him, or his parents.

He swung the ax into the chopping block and left it there and walked to the lakeside where a small shingle beach edged the bright blue waters of the lake. A few ducks half swam, half flew away, quacking noisily at the intrusion. From here, he could see the whole end of the lake, including, if he'd wanted to, Lizzi's house. But he didn't look that way.

He stripped off his jeans and waded into the cold water and dived in, relishing its chill. The hot summer sun wasn't able to penetrate the icy depth of the snow-fed lake. The shock of the water against the heat of his body momentarily numbed the pain he felt at the memory of his sister's death for which he'd always feel responsible. And numbed the pain of Lizzi's anger.

He surfaced and looked straight at Lizzi's house in the distance, took in another deep lungful of air and kicked down to the bottom of the lake and swam underwater, watching the quicksilver flicks of a fish's tail as it swam behind some trailing weeds. The water was as clear and fresh as the air above. It was this he craved—absolution, a new beginning. He needed to re-find his innocence—his faith in himself and in other people. But how could he have faith in himself if the woman he loved didn't trust him?

He closed his eyes and let himself drift up to the surface. But why should she? He'd known she wanted to be independent and yet he'd let his protective instincts override that knowledge. She was right. His need to protect had been stronger than his respect for her. Wouldn't he ever learn?

The sun was still hot, the snow-capped mountains still pristine against the vivid blue sky. If he couldn't learn here, he couldn't learn anywhere.

He changed course with the same agility as the fish and swam to shore. Naked, he walked up to his house with its uncompromising stone facade, punctured with walls of glass, and turned around and looked hard at Lizzi's house.

He'd learn; he'd make sure of it. There had to be some mid-point between her need for independence and his need to protect the people he cared for. He'd go to Lizzi and they'd work it out. Because there was no way he was going to lose Lizzi as he'd lost his sister.

———

It was after five in the afternoon the following day, and the café was still busy. Lizzi sat in her office, poring over her laptop, checking and re-checking her finances, trying to work out where she could make more savings, trying to figure out how she could bring in more business. But the earthquake had seemingly dried up overseas inquiries for the time being. And it was here and now she needed the money.

For the first time in a long time, she felt helpless. She sighed and rested her aching head in her hands, trying to figure out how she could take control of her café once more and move forward with her business.

And not only the café. She also needed to take control of her life. And to do that she needed to unravel her complex feelings toward Pete.

Suddenly, above the hum of voices in the café, she

heard one which made her sit up straight. She couldn't see Pete from where she was, but she recognized his voice. Despite what she *wanted* to feel, the smooth, deep tone curled its way somewhere deep inside and gave a little tug.

She jumped up and re-positioned her laptop. There was no way she was going to let him get to her. This was going to be purely a business discussion.

When she opened the door, Pete stood there with his usual smart shirt, open at the neck and his jeans. But without his usual smile. She stepped to one side to allow him to pass. She'd never seen him look so serious before.

"Pete," she acknowledged.

He nodded in response and strode over to the window, flung it open and walked onto the deck. She walked up behind him, noticing how tightly he gripped the railings.

"Are you okay?"

He glanced at her, again no smile. "Sure," he said in a clipped way. "You?"

"Yeah. Can I get you a drink? Tea, coffee?"

"No, thanks."

"Beer then?"

"Sure. Whatever."

She nodded, flashing a quick, uncertain smile. She walked quickly to the sideboard and pulled a beer from the small fridge and twisted off the cap. She glanced at his silhouette, dark and powerful against the rich afternoon sunlight. She'd never seen him like this before. She hesitated and then grabbed a bottle for herself. She walked over to him. Close up she could see the muscles working in his jaw. He was as tense as a coiled spring.

"Pete," she said, tentatively offering him the bottle. He turned slowly, took it and placed it on the table.

"I need to tell you why I did what I did. I'll tell you quickly because it's not something I like to dwell on." He paused, but she didn't interrupt. She could see the effort it was taking to focus on what he had to say. "My sister, Alitia. You knew she was five years younger than me and died overseas when she was twenty-two, four years ago. What I didn't tell you is how it happened."

"Are you sure you want to tell me?"

"Yes, I'm sure. At nineteen, Alitia went overseas and stayed there. No amount of reasoning or cajoling would make her agree that traveling through India with only her charm to protect her was risky."

There was a long pause which Lizzi knew not to break. She could see Pete wanted to continue; she could see the pain in his face.

"But she wasn't charming enough to stop herself from being attacked, robbed and left for dead. We didn't find out where she was for weeks, and then she died in an over-crowded hospital in central India in my arms. And I'll never forgive myself." The words tumbled out of Pete's mouth as if he couldn't bear their taste.

Lizzi's legs nearly gave out from under her and she fell, rather than sat, into the nearest chair, shaking her head in disbelief. "That's terrible..." She felt chilled and sick at what Pete had said, not least because of the matter-of-fact way he'd stated it.

She looked up at him, tears springing to her eyes at the sight of his own tear-filled eyes. "I had no idea." She tried to reach for his hand, but he moved away, paced over to the railing and looked out over the water. He didn't look at her, but spoke into the still heat.

"Of course you wouldn't. My parents and I decided not

to tell anyone. There was no point and we couldn't bear to talk about it. It destroyed my father. He stopped living. Stopped working, stopped seeing people. He died within a year. The doctors said a heart attack. All my mother and I knew was that it was heart-related. An attack, or broken. It was the same deal. He was dead and my mother and I were bereft. So I stayed on Waiheke Island with Mum until she died last year." He sighed and was silent.

"I'm so sorry."

When she lifted her head, he was facing her. "I don't want your sympathy, Lizzi," he said in a stony voice that shot through her like a knife. "What I want is for you to understand why I wanted to help you."

She nodded. "You were trying to make sure I was all right in a way you couldn't for Alitia."

"Which I chose *not* to do for Alitia because I let her persuade me otherwise." His gaze was still hard on hers. "She's dead because I let her have her own way."

"But she wasn't a child, Pete. There was nothing more you could have done."

He shook his head helplessly. "There must have been something." He looked at her, and she felt the pain in his eyes as if it were her own. He shrugged. "Anyway, that's it. That's my story. I wanted you to know."

"Thank you for telling me. I do understand why you acted as you did. But you have to understand that I need to do this on my own. I can't have someone coming in and taking over... like in the past."

"And I won't." He came and sat opposite her. "But I still want to help you make a success of your business—and I want you to accept my help. Can you do that?"

"I don't want your money."

"I'm not talking about money. Listen to me. We both

want the same thing... for you to succeed. It's simply the tactics which we don't agree on." He drew in a deep breath. "How about we work out a way for you to succeed in which we can both work together?"

She nodded. "Okay, let's talk it through."

He sat back, sighed and picked up his beer and took a swig. He suddenly looked exhausted. There were shadows under his eyes, and Lizzi realized what telling her his private grief had cost him. When he looked at her, she noticed the expression in his eyes had changed, too.

She felt a sharp stab of regret that the lingering warmth she was used to seeing there when he looked at her, had disappeared. And she'd made it go. She just hoped she could also make it return some day. She cleared her throat.

He took another swig of beer, his eyes never leaving hers. "You start. Tell me what you need. Because this isn't about money, is it?"

She shook her head. "I need to succeed at this. I need to show... my father, Charles, and... not least, myself... that I can do this."

He didn't ask any more questions, simply looked her steadily in the eye, his mouth a determined, tense line. "Okay. So what's your plan?"

"The overseas inquiries have dried up overnight." She twisted her laptop to face him. "Email after email of cancelations." She sighed. "So it's the domestic market and visitors who've come to New Zealand despite the recent earthquakes I need to appeal to. Passing traffic. But it's not enough." She walked over to the function room. "This is underutilized. If I employed a chef I could open in the evenings, too. But there are other restaurants and there's no reason for people to come to us instead. The overnight visitors in Shelter Springs are limited by accommodation."

"What about the new motel being built?"

"They'll have their own restaurant."

"So, make sure yours has a point of difference."

She frowned. "What do you have in mind?"

They talked into the evening, sustained by café leftovers and a bottle of wine, poring over spreadsheets, marketing plans, brainstorming different ideas. It wasn't until the early hours that they came up with a plan.

Pete looked up from the notes and spreadsheet on the computer. "It'll work."

Lizzi poured herself a coffee and leaned against the counter. "It should do, shouldn't it?" She brought him a coffee and placed it on the table. She looked over his shoulder at the laptop, absently placing her hand on his shoulder. He stilled.

"I reckon it will," he said. "Don't try to be everything to all people, work on your strengths and differences. People will pay for that."

"Are you sure? Are you willing to pull your top wines from the venues in the South Island and focus them here, in the café?"

He shrugged. "I won't be losing so much. The previous winemaker only had a toe-hold in the market, enough to see what the potential could be if we transferred it to The Lakehouse Café." He looked up and smiled. "Exclusive purveyors of fine wines."

She laughed, and without thinking, she leaned over and kissed him. They parted, and he gripped her shoulder. She hardly dared to breathe, wondering if he was going to pull her closer to him, *wanting* him to pull her closer. But then...

her breathe hitched in her throat as he pushed her gently away.

His eyes narrowed. "What are you doing, Lizzi? Or more to the point, why?"

She swallowed and stepped away, pushing her hair out of her eyes. "I'm sorry. I guess I got carried away."

He carefully pushed her hair from her face. "I want you, you know I do. But I can't get close to you one minute, only to be pushed away the next." His voice was gentle, and she could still see arousal in his eyes, but his tone was firm. "I don't want any guesses about our future together. Tell me when you know for sure. Okay?" He smiled briefly before moving away.

"I'm sorry," she repeated. "I—"

"Forget it," he said, walking toward the door.

She frowned. Forget it? Forget that kiss? There was no way that she was going to forget it. How could he leave after that?

"You're going?" Even as she said the words, she realized how dumb they sounded. And, by the expression on his face, so did he.

"Yes, I'm going. Collecting my keys and walking to the door is the usual prelude to leaving."

"Of course. Look, I'm sorry..."

He held up his hand again. "There's nothing to be sorry for. We made good progress tonight. Let's leave it at that, okay?"

"Okay."

"Goodnight, then."

"Night." She followed him to the door and stood holding on to it, watching as he drove off into the night. She closed the door and tried to unravel the threads of relief and excitement at the business plans they'd put in place, all

mixed up with the bitter disappointment and embarrassment of having been refused a second kiss.

A kiss, she thought as she looked in the mirror at her
confused face, which she hadn't known she'd wanted quite
so much until that moment. And which she wondered if
she'd be able to get over quite as easily as Pete so obviously
had.

CHAPTER ELEVEN

It had to happen.

The weeks passed by in a whirl of busyness. Between running the café, planning for the future, looking after Aimee and trying to figure out what to do about Pete, Lizzi had pushed Charles to the back of her mind.

Charles hadn't contacted her since his arrival, but she'd heard he'd come into Shelter Springs for supplies from time to time. But he'd made no attempt to see her, or Aimee. He hadn't even rung them.

She'd told Aimee that her father had returned to the family home, but Aimee hadn't responded. She'd shown no interest which hadn't surprised Lizzi.

So when the bell of the café jangled one morning, and Charles entered, Lizzi froze with surprise. Her first instinct was to look for Aimee. Damn, she was alone behind the counter.

"Charles." Lizzi nodded, not approaching him. "I wasn't expecting you."

"Elizabeth," he said with equal coolness.

"How are things at the house?"

"I've just about wound things up. I was looking through some photos and thought of Aimee."

She raised an eyebrow. "You've only just thought of her now?"

He shrugged. "I've been busy. And I found a letter from Mum for you." He handed her the letter.

"So... when are you leaving?"

"That's not very welcoming, now is it?"

"No. When are you leaving?" she repeated, her fear making her firmer.

"In a few days. I've sorted through the house and put it on the market."

Lizzi felt a twinge of regret. The old homestead and estate had been in Charles's family for generations, but, apparently, it didn't mean so much to him. "Mission accomplished, then."

"Yes." He glanced at Aimee who hadn't yet noticed him. "But before I go, I'd like Aimee to come to the estate. There are some things Mum wanted her to have."

Lizzi's mouth dried. "Can't you bring them here?"

"No. Besides, I want her to see the old place."

"She's seen it. We visited your mother often."

His eyes hardened. "I want her to come, Elizabeth. If she doesn't, I'll simply come and get her."

She shook her head. "No, you won't."

"Good, then, I'll see you both at six tomorrow night." He looked over to Aimee. "Aimee!" he called, and Aimee looked up, and her happy face immediately fell. "Come here!"

Aimee froze. Lizzi stepped forward and extended her hand. "Come here, darling. Your Dad wants to say hello."

Tentatively Aimee stepped forward and grabbed Lizzi's

hand like a lifeline. Aimee took a step away and looked up at Charles.

"Daddy," she said uncertainly.

"Aimee." His tone was even, unemotional.

Lizzi's heart broke for Aimee, but she was reassured by Charles's tone. Cool was preferable to aggressive.

"And have you been good since I've been away?"

What kind of question was that? "Of course she's been good," Lizzi snapped.

"I'd like to hear Aimee answer for herself."

Aimee shrunk closer to Lizzi and nodded.

"I didn't hear you, Aimee."

Aimee looked up at Lizzi with big watery eyes. Lizzi nodded, encouragingly. "Daddy's about to leave, darling. Just tell him how you've been."

Lizzi's heart wrenched as she saw the effort Aimee exerted to stand a little taller and face her father. "I've been good, Daddy," she said in a quiet voice.

"Good. Then you can come to the house, and I'll give you the things Grandma left for you tomorrow night."

Aimee's lip trembled as she nodded.

Charles grunted, and he glanced at Lizzi. "She hasn't grown much, has she?"

Lizzi could have screamed at Charles. Instead, she calmly put her arm around Aimee and turned her away from Charles. "Why don't you go into the kitchen, find some marshmallows I've put in the drawer, and we'll have a hot chocolate?"

Aimee didn't need asking twice, and she shot off. Lizzi turned to Charles. "Don't you ever talk to my daughter like that again."

Charles's lip quirked in a show of amusement. "And what would you do if I did?" His eyes narrowed. He chuckled. "It would be worth doing simply to see your reaction. I think I'd like that. Tomorrow night. And make sure you show up. Otherwise, I'll come here for you both."

Before Lizzi could respond, he'd walked out the door without a backward glance.

Lizzi pushed a shaky hand through her hair and was about to walk through to the office when a chair scraped back from the closest table, hidden behind an old-fashioned coat rack, and Pete appeared.

"Pete! I didn't see you there."

He rose and came over to her. "I called in to see how things were going."

"Fine. Since our meeting at the bank, everything's going well. The new evening business is slowly increasing, ahead of projected—"

He put out his hand to stop her. "Good. But tell me one thing."

"What?"

"Tell me why Aimee recoiled from Charles like that. Tell me why Aimee didn't want to go anywhere near him."

It was like an icy hand gripped Lizzi's heart—simply reached in and grabbed it and squeezed. She rubbed her chest with the heel of her hand and stepped away.

"Tell me, Lizzi." His voice was quiet and insistent.

She bit her lip and looked away.

"Tell me." His voice was quieter, and yet more demanding.

She shook her head.

"I'll go then and leave you to your secrets." He took a few steps away before turning back to her. "You know, secrets aren't good for people."

"Sometimes they're necessary."

"No, they're never necessary. You should be more open.

Hell, you should shout to the world what you're thinking, what you're feeling. You shouldn't be afraid because I reckon the world would like to know more about the real Lizzi Burnett."

He didn't wait for an answer and she watched him leave but was powerless to stop him. Because he was right. She did have secrets. And she was so used to keeping them close that it had become second nature. But the secrets were driving the wedge between them deeper and deeper. When would the connection between them finally split apart? How much longer could it continue?

She went into her office and tapped her mother-in-law's letter on the desk, nervous about opening it. She'd been close to Margaret and had made sure she and Aimee visited often, particularly during the last weeks of her life.

She opened the envelope to find a couple of pages of shakily written words. She read them slowly, frowning as she tried to control the emotions which the words stirred in her. They were her mother-in-law through and through—words of love, of practicality and finally words of wisdom, for her alone.

She jumped up and wiped her eyes at the old lady's final words—words which she now remembered Margaret had said to her just before she died. She'd dismissed them then. But now?

It was classical music Pete always listened to when he wanted to think clearly. There was something about its patterns which helped unravel his thoughts. But it wasn't his thoughts tonight. He needed to *understand* Lizzi which was proving a challenge.

When the soft knock at the door came, he didn't hear it, so immersed was he in his thoughts and the music.

But by the third time, the knock had got louder, and he looked up suddenly. He placed his glass of whiskey onto the side table, walked toward the door and opened it.

Lizzi stood outside, her dark hair lit by the moonlight. "Beethoven?" she asked, as if that explained her sudden appearance at his door at one in the morning.

It took him a minute to believe that the object of his thoughts only moments earlier had somehow materialized outside his door.

"Lizzi?"

"Sorry it's so late, but I saw your light was on and..."

"And? What?"

She took a deep breath. "Thought I'd come over."

He opened the door wide. She stepped inside the shadowy room which was illuminated by a single side light.

He closed the door quietly behind her, leaned against it, and watched her walk over to the far side of the room. There was something different about her tonight. Something quiet, hesitant. He could see it in the way she held herself and looked around. As if she was lost somehow.

"What's happened?" he asked.

Her shoulders tensed but she didn't turn around. She drew in a deep breath and picked up the CD case. "I didn't know you liked Beethoven."

"There's a lot you don't know about me." He paused, wondering if he should give her time. But for once he didn't want to give her time. "What's happened?" he repeated. "Why are you here?"

She shifted slightly, and at that moment the moon shone and he saw the tears in her eyes. He reached for her and brought her to him. "What's happened?"

"My mother-in-law told me something the day she died which I shrugged off, thinking her words were too sentimental to apply to me. But she obviously thought they were important—so important that she wrote them in a letter which Charles delivered today. I'd almost forgotten them."

"And what was that?"

"That life without love is a cold thing. It becomes an endurance test rather than a delight to be savored." She lifted her face to his, and he could see the tears clearly now. "Pete, I don't want to be cold any more. I don't want to endure my life. I want to *live* it, savor it."

Still, he didn't move.

"Pete? Pete?" The sob hung on her words, unanswered, until he took her hand and pulled her into the bedroom.

Lizzi might have come to him, she might have practically asked for love, but from the moment Pete took her hand, *he* was in control.

He led her into the bedroom, and turned her in his arms and kissed her with a kiss that held everything she wanted so desperately—love, tenderness, passion and, not least, for the moment, oblivion. She wanted to forget the fear she felt in the presence of the father of her child; and wanted to give everything she had to the man who kept on giving, despite everything she'd done to drive him away.

She surrendered all thought under the sureness of his kiss, melting against his body whose strength supported her totally. And she needed that strength now above all things. She wanted to suspend her thoughts and feelings and give herself to someone who would take the lead and simply love her, without questions, without agenda, without demands.

And he did. From the touch of his fingers as they drew

up inside her arm and hooked off her cardigan with one smooth flowing motion, to the gentle brush of his lips on her eyelids, sweeping away the tears, he gave her what she craved.

Slowly, tenderly, he undressed her, until she stood naked in front of him.

"You are so beautiful, Lizzi." He reached out and swept the side of her breasts with his finger, and she gasped at the sudden blast of arousal. She was shaking when he drew her into his arms.

She clung to him as he lifted her onto the bed, laid her head on the pillow, smoothed out her hair and kissed her tenderly on the lips. When he left her, she rose, needing his touch in some basic scientific way, like a flower following the sun, or the tides being pulled and pushed by the moon.

But before she could reach him, he'd returned, naked, to the bed and she fell back with a sigh as he swept his hands up her outstretched arms and held them open, while he pinned her hips with his own. Trapped in position, he lowered his mouth to hers and kissed her, teasing her lips open, finding her tongue with his, and forcing her to suspend all thought, to accept only feeling—of skin on skin and his body within hers.

Pete awoke to a deep sense of peace. For a moment he couldn't think where he was. But not for one minute did he forget *who* he was with. He looked around for Lizzi and didn't have to look far to see her sitting on the other side of the bed. No one could make him feel this way. So... complete and at peace.

The darkness had melted away, but sunrise was still an hour away. Lizzi sat, looking out the window toward Shelter

Springs, her outline rimmed with the strange, unearthly pale gray that was neither night nor day. And he knew he'd lost that intimacy of the previous night. He could see it in the set of her shoulders.

He sighed, watching the shadows of the branches of the towering beech tree which grew outside the window, move across the ceiling.

She turned toward him. "You're awake."

He rolled onto his side and reached out for her hand. He thrust his fingers through hers and curled them around. "Yeah."

"I hope I didn't disturb you."

She withdrew her hand, buttoned up her top. It was only then that he realized she was already dressed.

He rose and pulled on some jeans. The time for nakedness had gone. "No, you didn't wake me." He walked over to the window and looked out across the lake, hands on hips.

"Good." She sighed, and he heard her rise and walk over to him. He closed his eyes as he inhaled her perfume and held his breath, waiting for her touch. But it didn't come. His first instincts had been correct.

He opened his eyes and looked at her. There were dark shadows under her eyes. She looked exhausted. All hurt and anger vanished as he reached out to her. But she shook her head, and he thrust his hands in his pockets to hide his instinctive reaction.

"Didn't you sleep?"

A small grin crept over her delicate features. "You know I didn't."

"But after we made love?"

She shook her head. "My mind wouldn't stop racing."

"About what?"

"About Charles."

Pete didn't like the way she said her ex-husband's name —tentatively, as if she were hiding something. More secrets? The fact she still had feelings for him? Who knew? *He* certainly didn't and it was grinding him down.

"You haven't told me why Aimee recoiled from Charles like that."

"No. But I will, I promise. Just not today."

He grunted with frustration. Why she was trying to protect Charles, was beyond him. "What's different about tomorrow?"

She looked up at him with a complex expression which he couldn't read—frowning and intense. "Charles will be gone."

He felt instant relief at her words. It was like a heavy thundercloud had lifted. "Thank God for that!" He took her hand and she pushed her fingers through his, and for a moment the veil was lifted. Then the frown returned and she pulled away.

"I have to go," she said.

"So early? At least have a coffee before you leave."

"No, I need to go back, sort out a few things before I pick up Aimee from Amber's, get her to school, go to the café. I've a lot on this morning."

There was more to it than that—he could see it in her eyes. He fisted his hands in frustration. He wanted to look after her, but he was powerless to do so. He watched as she picked up her things from around the bedroom, before standing uncertainly at the door, holding the handle of her bag in both hands.

"And Charles isn't planning on coming to the café today?"

She shook her head. "No."

"You sure?"

"Yes. He said he wasn't."

"Good. So Aimee won't see Charles before he leaves." Pete had to be sure.

"No, she won't."

So if she was sure Aimee wouldn't be seeing Charles, why was she so unsettled, so agitated? He could see it in her quick, awkward movements, in the twisting of her hands, the brief grimaces masking an inner struggle. But he couldn't help her, because ultimately she wouldn't allow him to.

"Good." He walked toward the door.

"Pete!" Lizzi called as she followed him. "Thank you, for last night."

"You're thanking me for sex?"

"No, I'm thanking you for being there for me."

"Of course. But I didn't realize it was a one-way street. I thought we were there for each other. Weren't we, Lizzi? Or are you backing off into friendship again? You know, sometimes, I get the dizzying sensation that I'm a yo-yo. Up one minute, and down the next. At some point, I have the uncanny feeling that the thread will break and I'll be cut loose. You can only play this game with me for so long."

"It's not a game. And I don't mean to be playing with you at all." She re-tied her hair into a tight ponytail as if that would make everything clear and ordered once more. "I wanted to be with you, and I thought you wanted me too."

"I do, but not like this. Not with you disappearing in the morning with a distance between us bigger than when you came. I don't understand why you need this distance, Lizzi. The only reason I can think of is to drive me away. Is that what you want?"

She shook her head, but her confusion was plain to see.

"No, of course not. Come over tomorrow night. We can talk then."

"Why not tonight? Look, we both have a lot on. How about we leave it until you've sorted things out?"

"Okay. If that's what you want."

"It's what *you* need."

He walked her to her car. She started the engine and wound down the window. "I'm sorry it's such a mess, Pete. But it'll all be over soon, I promise."

Before he could question her further, she was gone, driving along the rough track, toward the main road to Shelter Springs, the car's headlights forcing their way into the darkness ahead. And all the while her words repeated in his head.

It'll all be over.

She must be meaning Charles would have gone. But if she did, why didn't she say that?

It was a cloudy, blustery evening and the air crackled with electricity. The night was split with forked lightning, but there was no rain as yet. But Lizzi knew it would come. She had a deep sense of foreboding and twice on the drive over to Charles's, she'd given the instructions for her phone to dial Pete's number and twice she'd stopped it before it had connected.

She couldn't keep running to Pete for support because he always gave it without question, and then she inevitably pulled away as doubt and distrust crept in and taunted her again. And she felt a deep fear that he might be right. She might pull him in, only to find that the cord that connected them had broken. And she couldn't face that.

She turned into the drive of the grand old house and parked by the front door. Before she switched out the lights, she frowned. Charles had told her that the couple who looked after the house would be there, but there were no lights in the wing of the house which they occupied. She couldn't see their cars either. There was only Charles's car. But by then it had begun to rain—large drops smacked onto her windscreen, and she couldn't see clearly.

She got out and, raising her collar against the rain and the wind, walked quickly to the front door and knocked. There was no reply, but she could see through the glass that there was a light on in the drawing room at the rear of the house. Tentatively she opened the door and entered the house.

Immediately she was struck by a sense of emptiness. Everything looked just as it had before, but it didn't *feel* the same. She hesitated. She was simply projecting her feelings of loss over the death of Charles's mother, Margaret, that was all. She'd find Charles, get whatever he wanted to give to Aimee, and leave. Otherwise, he'd appear at the café, and she couldn't cope with that.

"Charles," she called, her voice sounding preternaturally loud in the wooden-floored hallway. She closed the front door and walked into the formal sitting room. Again, everything was in its place in the elegant room, but it no longer looked lived in, no longer cared for or loved. She shivered.

The old grandfather clock ticked the time away, as if nothing had changed. But everything had changed. She heard a movement behind her. She glanced around to find Charles standing tall, leaning against the door jamb.

She pressed her palm against her thumping heart.

"Charles! You startled me! Where is everyone? Why's the house in darkness?"

He didn't move for a moment, and she couldn't see him clearly in the shadowy room. Then he grunted a little and stepped away. "Drink?"

She wasn't surprised he didn't answer her questions; he'd always ignored anything said or done which was of no interest to him.

"No, thank you. I've come for the things you said Margaret wanted Aimee to have."

He poured himself a drink with his back to her. His powerful wide shoulders prompted memories of the man she'd fallen in love with, memories of the fun and passion of their early years together. He turned around, and all the good memories vanished.

"So... where is everyone?"

"I dismissed them. They're no longer required. The house has been sold to an overseas buyer who'll take possession in a month's time."

"That was quick."

"I wanted it settled, and what I want, I get. Although, Elizabeth, it looks as though you went against me this time."

She swallowed. "What do you mean?"

He opened his arms wide in mock confusion. "Where's Aimee? Where's my daughter, who I asked to see?"

"You must have known I wouldn't bring her here."

He placed the glass heavily onto the table. "I *told* you to bring her here, Elizabeth, and you disobeyed me."

Fear sliced through her. "I... I made a mistake coming here. Whatever you have for Aimee, leave it here. I still have a key. I'll collect it after you've gone."

He didn't move, simply stood there like a rock—between her and the door.

She tried to step around him, but he caught her arm. "You're not leaving." His eyes flashed.

She slipped her other hand into her pocket and fumbled for her phone. Thank goodness she hadn't left it in the car.

"Okay," she said trying to sound calm. "I'll stay. Maybe I *will* have that drink after all."

He grunted and reluctantly let go of her arm and went toward the decanter.

"No whiskey, thanks. Do you have wine?"

"It's in the fridge." He began to top up his suddenly empty glass, and her heart sank. Charles sober was scary; Charles drunk was terrifying. "Help yourself. I'll be waiting."

He sat and watched her as she went into the kitchen, fumbling for her phone as she walked across the tiled floor. She opened the fridge and took her phone, entered the passcode and began to search for Pete's number. She found it as the fridge door opened wide and Charles looked at the phone. He took the phone from her and slammed it into the fridge and closed the door.

"I couldn't trust you before and, it seems, I can't now."

CHAPTER TWELVE

P ete was on his bed, watching the storm play out across the lake. He frowned as his phone went again. What was Lizzi playing at, trying to call him? Hadn't he made it plain he didn't want a relationship until she was sure about her feelings? And why did she stop the calls within seconds of making them?

He swung his legs onto the floor and sat for a few seconds considering the phone. Then he pressed redial and walked across to the window and looked out across the rain-lashed lake toward her house which he couldn't see through the low cloud.

The phone rang and rang. Why wouldn't she answer when she'd obviously just used her phone? He stopped the call and glanced at the time. It was gone ten. Strange time to call, particularly after how they'd parted. But he had a bad feeling about this.

He rang the café, then her cottage, then her cell again. Nothing. Then he had a thought and sent a text to Gemma at Glencoe who confirmed Lizzi had dropped Aimee off with her a few hours before. After a little hesitation, she told him where Lizzi had been going.

He wasted no time in dressing and heading off toward Shelter Springs, out to the Burnett homestead, hoping he wasn't too late.

"Who are you trying to call?" Charles repeated, as he grabbed her wrist.

"Charles, you're hurting me," she said as the grip on her wrist grew tighter.

"Who were you trying to call, Elizabeth?"

"Only a friend. Pete, you know, you met him."

"Pete," he spat out. "Are you close with this Pete?"

"Yes, no, I don't know," she replied.

"Tell me the truth."

"Yes, I'm close to Pete. Charles, I'm free to be with who I like, just as you're with Maria. We're not married anymore, Charles. You know that."

But from the cold frown he wore, she could see that he'd gone past the point of reason.

"Is Aimee even my daughter?"

"Yes, of course, she is."

"Tell me the truth."

"I am. Please, let go, you're hurting me, Charles."

"Not before you tell me the truth."

"I *am* telling you the truth. Don't you remember anything? Don't you remember the love we once shared? How we made love all the time because we were young and in love? And how happy we were when I became pregnant? Don't you remember any of that?" Her voice cracked with emotion as she tried to contain the grief which she'd suppressed for so long—grief that the man she'd fallen in love with hadn't really existed.

She cocked her head to one side, trying to make him see reason with her expression alone. Trying to communicate the truth and force of her emotion with her eyes. For a brief moment, she thought she'd got through to him, and he relaxed his grip. But before she could slip her hands away, he'd tightened it again, and his expression had become like a stone mask.

"I don't believe a word you're saying. You didn't bring Aimee to me. Why wouldn't you bring a daughter to meet her own father?"

"You know why. You hurt her once, not just with your indifference, you know you did. I can't risk letting you near her again."

"You're lying. I simply disciplined her, like any good father should. No, there's more to it than that. I always thought she was weak, nothing like me. I'm not her real father, am I?"

She shook her head in denial, terrified by the turn of events.

"I don't know why I didn't see it before. She doesn't even look like me."

"She has your eyes," Lizzi gulped. "She has your coloring. Charles, believe me, she *is* your daughter."

"I'm sick of your lies, Elizabeth. You know I don't tolerate lies."

"I've never lied to you." She had to think. "Let me show you some photos. There's one of you as a baby, and you're the spitting image of Aimee. Let me show you." She glanced at the door to the study. There was a phone in there. If she could only get to it, she could get help. "I'll get them, and I'll show you."

He grunted and threw her hand away, causing her to stumble. He strode over to the whiskey decanter and poured himself yet another. "Go on then. Get the damn photos. They'll prove she's not my child." He swore before knocking back another drink. "I'm relieved not to have such a scrawny brat for a daughter."

She took her opportunity and stumbled toward the door, out across the hallway and into the study. Heart thumping, she looked around for the phone, quietly picked it up and dialed Pete's number. *Please pick up. Please pick up.* But it rang and rang. Then it was answered.

"Hello?"

"Pete?" But before she could say anything further the phone was snatched away and torn from its socket, and thrown across the room, breaking a window as it landed.

"You're a deceitful bitch, Elizabeth. You were ringing him, weren't you? Your boyfriend. Aimee's father." His eyes were dark with hate, his face inflamed with whiskey and anger. The last thing she saw was his raised hand aimed directly at her, and the last thing she felt was the pain that shot through her as his fist connected with her body and she slammed to the floor.

***

The storm crashed around the valley as Pete drove his car through the intense darkness, relieved only by flashes of lightning. Pete threw the phone onto the passenger seat. Another call, cut short. Except this time she called his name. What the hell was going on? And what on earth was she playing at, coming up here all alone? Pure, unadulterated fear for her life was vented into anger, focused on getting to where she was, as quickly as he could.

The car bounced on the pitted surface of the road leading to the Burnett estate, which had fallen into disrepair. He peered up ahead of the winding road, whose huge trees bent and swayed in the surging winds, revealing lights in the downstairs of the house.

Some instinct made him park the car just out of sight of the house. No need to advertise his arrival. Adrenaline surging, he walked past an un-curtained window and stopped, reassured by what he saw. Charles sat nursing a whiskey, his eyes closed—for all the world enjoying a quiet night of relaxation.

Pete was relieved. Maybe all was well. Charles was acting as if everything were normal, that nothing was untoward. And then Charles moved his leg, pushing something with his foot and said something.

Pete gripped the windowsill as he followed Charles's gaze, toward a figure who lay unmoving on the floor. He leaned in, straining to make sense of the shadows. Then he saw rich chestnut hair shining under the light of a lamp. The figure moved under Charles's insistent nudging foot, revealing a face—Lizzi's face resting on her hand—from which a dark line flowed. It was only when Pete traced the line to a white rug that he realized what it was—blood.

He roared, pushed himself away from the house and raced to the front door. And, with no more thought about caution, burst into the study and launched himself at the unsuspecting Charles, who'd risen out of the chair at the sound. Catching him off guard, Pete landed a punch that sent Charles to the floor.

With Charles lying, unmoving, Pete raced to Lizzi and gently pushed her hair from her face. With relief, he saw her eyelids flutter.

"Lizzi! Can you hear me?"

She opened her eyes once before grimacing. He pressed a cushion to her head where her bloody hand rested. "Hold it there." She groaned but did as he said, closing her eyes tight.

It was all he could do for her for the moment. He had other matters to attend to. He glanced at Charles. Lizzi would be okay, he'd make sure of that. Unlike Charles who, unless he got out of Pete's sight immediately, most definitely would *not* be okay.

Charles came round with a groan and looked up at them both.

"You coward, Charles!" spat Pete. "What the hell have you done to her?"

"Me?" Charles rubbed his cheek and sat up. "Nothing. And nor"—he rose slowly to his feet—"will you." Without warning, he launched himself at Pete, knocking him to the ground. Charles drew back his fist but Pete rolled to one side, and Charles's fist only glanced off his body. Pete was filled with total fury, as he jumped to his feet. He didn't feel the follow-up punch Charles made which connected with his cheek. He simply waited for his best shot—a well-placed left hook on Charles's chin—which did what Pete wanted, sent Charles flying backward.

Pete stood over him, his fist ready to throw another punch, breathing heavily. "Had enough yet?"

Charles rolled over and rose unsteadily to his feet. "No way."

It was all Pete needed to hear before launching another well-placed blow to Charles's jaw which sent him reeling to the ground again—this time unmoving.

Lizzi tried to stand, the cushion still pressed to her head.

"Pete! What have you done?"

Pete rubbed his hand, injured by the blows he'd given Charles. "What have *I* done? Knocked him senseless, I hope."

"My head hurts," she groaned.

Pete picked up the phone. "I'll call an ambulance."

"There's no point. It'll be ages before anyone's here."

Lizzi gingerly touched her forehead and winced. "I just need some ice," she said, as she walked carefully out the door. He helped her into the kitchen and had her seated with an icepack when he heard the sound of a car roaring up the drive and then footsteps.

Callum burst into the room. "Pete!" said Callum, kneeling over a moaning Charles. "What the hell happened here?"

"It's Lizzi, she's in the kitchen. She needs medical attention." Callum went through to Lizzi.

Pete made a mistake then. He turned his back on Charles, watching to make sure Lizzi was okay. The last thing Pete saw was Charles's fist, a split-second before it made contact with his face, and then everything went blank.

Pete awoke suddenly to find himself alone with Lizzi, who was kneeling beside him. He reached out and grabbed her hand firmly in his. The effort made his head pound. He grimaced.

"Pete," she half-sobbed. "I was so afraid..."

His head throbbed and trying to think was like trying to aim at a moving target. He swore under his breath.

"*Pete*, are you okay?"

It was Lizzi's voice, but for the life of him he couldn't seem to focus on her face. "Sure," he said, but he'd never been more unsure of anything in his life. His head felt like it'd been used for a rugby ball and his mouth was parched. "I need water. I'm so damned thirsty."

His request was met with a stifled, relieved laugh. "Sure. Stay there. Don't move and I'll get you a glass."

He pushed himself off the floor and staggered a little. He gripped the chair and took a deep breath. He could do this. He felt his temple which was already swollen. Man, Charles knew how to fight. Then he remembered.

"Lizzi!"

She came running with a glass of water.

"Where's Charles?" Pete asked.

"Morgan arrived just after Callum, and he's taken him away. Callum's in the house somewhere gathering Charles's things."

"Away?"

"To hospital and then, if he's okay to travel, they're making sure he leaves the country."

"About time!" Then he remembered. "Your head! Let me see." He walked carefully toward her and held her head in his hands as he examined her.

She lifted a hand roughly wrapped in a bandage through which blood seeped. "I banged my head and was out for a few seconds, but it was my hand which got cut up on the glass table which shattered when I fell on it."

He took her hand and the sight of her blood inflamed his own. He shook his head, ignoring the increased throbbing. "How could you risk yourself, Lizzi? What were you thinking, coming here alone?"

"I had no choice."

"You should have told me, damn it!" He dropped her hand and looked at her questioningly, but she made no attempt to answer.

He stepped away, sighed and gripped the chair until his knuckles went white.

"Why didn't you tell me? Didn't you trust me? You'd rather put yourself in danger than ask me for help? Do you think you're the only person who can solve your problems?"

"Don't you stand there and tell me what I should or shouldn't have done! I did what I thought best. Like I've always done." Her voice was dangerously low. "Don't you dare judge me! *No* one can know what I've been through, what it was like, trying to keep my head above water, the café running, Aimee safe while trying to hide the cuts and bruises which he gave me at night."

"I can't know, but I can guess. You still should have trusted me."

Lizzi paced the floor, frowning at the stylized red flowers on the white rug, as if they held the secret to her thoughts. "I kept Charles's violence secret from everyone except a few close friends because I didn't want to destroy his mother's life or make him even worse in Aimee's eyes." She shook her head, her focus not deviating from the rug, as she wiped away a tear. "I was *so* young. I had no idea what to do! I had no idea who to turn to!" She flung her arms wide. "If I knew a woman like that now, who was suffering as I had, I'd tell her to go to the cops, to get out and hide while the law did what they had to do." She wiped her face with her sleeve and twisted around to look at him, and he felt his heart burn with rage for what the woman he loved had suffered.

"Lizzi..."

She held up her hand awkwardly, determined to go on. "But I didn't do that. I didn't think anyone would believe me. Because how could my handsome, strong Charles whose family was one of the original founding families in the area, so upright, so entrenched in the community, be a wife beater? He was a hero, goddamn it! But I should have told the world, regardless of the effect on his mother, on Aimee. I might not have told anyone then, but I made sure Maria—Charles's new wife—knew, but she didn't believe me." She shrugged. "And maybe he's not violent toward her. Just to me."

"I'm sorry, I'm so sorry that he did this to you, to Aimee. But that's the past. You have to move on. You have to learn to trust again."

"You don't understand."

"I understand perfectly. You didn't trust me, Lizzi. You didn't trust me," he repeated trying to drive home the truth to her. "I've bent over backward to prove to you that you can. But I realize now that you'll never change. You couldn't trust me with the truth about Charles, and what he's done, and you certainly don't trust me with yourself. There's always a barrier, isn't there? And I'm only now realizing it's a barrier that's serving a purpose."

"What purpose? What are you talking about?"

"You've no idea, have you? No idea that you're still trying to protect yourself from hurt. I know your father hurt you. I know Charles hurt you. And what I also know is that I *won't* hurt you. But you don't trust me enough to let that barrier go. There will always be secrets, won't there? Because they're part of the building blocks of the wall that protects you. You mistake the barrier for strength, for independence. But, you know what, Lizzi? Sometimes it takes strength to be in a relationship, to claim what you want and to make it work. And I don't know if you have that strength. And I don't know if I want to wait around, simply hoping you have, anymore."

He stepped away, and she reached out to him, but he stepped away again before she could touch him.

"I don't—I can't—"

"Don't say anything, Lizzi. You don't have to. I've said it all. The ambulance is here; you should go and get your head checked out."

Callum entered the room. "Lizzi?"

"I'm coming. Pete, you should get checked out too."

"No, I'm fine. I'll go straight home."

"I'll drive you home, Pete," said Callum. "Just to be sure."

"Okay." Pete turned to Lizzi. "Just go, Lizzi. Go."

From the ambulance she watched Callum close up the house and start the car. As the ambulance's headlights swung around the drive, they briefly illuminated Pete's face as he looked up at her. Then it was gone.

Was he right? Was everything she'd believed a lie she'd devised through some deep-seated need to protect herself from hurt? If he was right, then it must be buried so deep that she hardly recognized it. But then, it had started when she was tiny. She'd never been quite enough for her father—not sporty enough, not academic enough. But she'd doggedly held on to the things she'd loved, like cooking, and had blocked off his derision as best she could. The wall that Pete had referred to. She closed her eyes as the ambulance bounced over the rutted track.

She closed her eyes more tightly still and remembered scenes like snapshots, except this time she was looking on, watching her, not *being* her, and she realized with slow clarity that Pete was right, which left only one thing to do. And that was to act. Because gone were the days when she'd simply build a higher wall to stave off the hurt. No, she wasn't that woman any more. She'd become the strong, independent woman she'd always wanted to be. And, through Pete's love, she'd also become someone who could love without reserve.

She drew in a shaky breath and slowly formulated a plan.

CHAPTER THIRTEEN

A week later and Pete had recovered from his concussion and was back at work, Charles had left the country, and everything had returned to normal.

But it wasn't the normal that Pete had hoped for or imagined a few weeks earlier. Instead of being with Lizzi, he sat alone in his office, tapping an old-fashioned invitation he'd received through the mail against his desk.

It was from Gemma and Callum Mackenzie—an invitation to their Easter party. He propped the gold-embossed invitation against his computer. He couldn't remember the last time he'd received such a thing. His social life was governed by texts, emails, Facebook, phone, any kind of social and electronic media, but not expensively produced invitations sent through the postal system.

When Gemma had mentioned the party to him in passing, he'd been non-committal. He'd said all he needed to say to Lizzi at Charles's house. There was nothing more to be added, nothing more to be gained by seeing her again.

He moved his finger along the scalloped edge of the card and couldn't help but smile. There was something so wonderfully traditional about it, something that reminded him of the interior of The Lakehouse Café, the sitting room in Lizzi's cottage, even the bedroom, where an antique satin dressing gown hung on the picture rail, appreciated for its beauty rather than its use.

That's what this place was like, he reminded himself. And that's partly why he'd been drawn to it. It had an old-fashioned quality. It could have been the warmth of the people and how they came together as a community, or maybe it was simply the unspoiled splendor of the Mackenzie Country. Whatever it was, he felt it was all somehow summed up in Lizzi.

He loved her, despite what he'd said to her. He loved her, and he couldn't resist an invitation to see her again. Even if they didn't speak, even if she avoided him, at least he'd see her. He sighed. He'd take what he could.

Glencoe was made for parties and the Mackenzie's annual Easter party was no exception. The grand nineteenth-century mansion, home to the Mackenzie family for over a hundred years, shone with myriad lights, whose effects were multiplied by the slanting beams of evening sunlight. The light from the large chandelier which dominated the room, bounced off the highly polished floorboards and deepened the rich hues of the Turkish rugs.

Gemma didn't believe in keeping fairy lights for Christmas, and they were strung everywhere—around the family portraits which hung on opulently wallpapered walls, giving the Mackenzie family's Victorian ancestors an almost festive air.

Lizzi laughed. Trust Gemma to add her quirky touch to

the grand homestead. She'd certainly loosened up the formal character of the house since she'd married Callum.

Lizzi gave another quick glance out the window. The lanterns in the trees cast their reflections into the lake below as other guests arrived, dressed to the nines in dinner jackets and long gowns. Jewelry sparkled at the throats of the women, catching the last rays of the sun as they walked into the house. Anyone who was anyone was here... except the person she wanted to see.

"Mum!" Aimee ran into the hall behind Gemma, making a bee-line for the Mackenzie kids and friends who gathered beside the two-story wooden staircase, which rose to an open gallery which ran the length of the rear of the grand old hall.

"Champagne?" Lizzi turned around to find Gemma holding out a Champagne flute to her.

"Please." Lizzi looked around. "This hall was made for celebrations."

"It's made for summer, all right. You try heating it in the middle of winter."

Lizzi smiled at the idea. Callum and Gemma Mackenzie were the richest landowners in the area. She'd never seen the Adam-style fireplace, around which inviting sofas were grouped, *not* without a wood fire in winter. Even now, in early autumn, the fire was lit and its crackle and piney fragrance filled the hall with a warm, welcoming ambiance.

Lizzi looked nervously around. "Is everybody here?"

"Nearly all the friends and neighbors we've invited have arrived. Only Dallas and Cassandra, and Lucia and Guy to come. Callum's flying them here. James will be with them. Seems he's fallen out with Susie, so she won't be here. Shame. I hope they get to work it out. She brought a different side out in him." She sipped her Champagne and looked around. "Now let's see, who else? Morgan and Rebecca are over there. And then there's Lady Mackenzie." Gemma rolled her eyes. "But I doubt you're referring to her."

Lizzi nodded but wasn't reassured. It seemed Gemma's sharp eyes missed nothing.

"But you don't mean any of those people, do you?"

"No." Lizzi took a deep breath. "Is Pete here?"

Gemma looked over Lizzi's shoulder. "He is now." She grinned. "He's just come in."

The roar of a plane landing drifted in through the open windows. Gemma's face lit up, and she ran outside to greet Callum and the others, barely able to contain her excitement.

Lizzi wondered if she'd ever experience such love and contentment, such a home as this, with a man with whom she shared her life completely. She walked over to greet Pete. But Aimee beat her to it and was swirling her new dress, with its full petticoats, for him to admire.

"Looking good, Miss Aimee."

"Thank you, Mr. Pete," she said with a cheeky grin.

He ruffled her hair. "Hey! Don't do that," she said, smoothing it down again. "I've just brushed it. I'm pretending it's been straightened."

He rolled his eyes and watched as she went running off. He turned to Lizzi with an expression which nearly broke her heart. "Hello, Lizzi."

"Hey, Pete. How have you been? How's your head?"

"Head's fine." He paused. "Thank you." He looked around, and she reached out to him and placed her hand on his arm. He stilled instantly.

"I have something to say."

"Go on."

"Later. The time's not right now."

He closed his eyes briefly and shook his head. Before he could respond, Callum, James, Dallas and Cassandra Mackenzie and their kids entered the room, together with Guy and Lucia, who was pregnant with twins. And then Rebecca began talking to Pete.

Lizzi moved away, helping Gemma to make sure everyone had what they needed. When she turned around, Pete was still listening to Rebecca, who was no doubt talking about the stars. Rebecca had been doing some research with him about planting vines according to the lunar and solar cycles. At first, Lizzi had thought Pete was only being polite when he expressed interest. But it seemed he *was* genuinely interested. Seemed her man had a soul that was less pragmatic than she'd thought. He was a strong man, yes. But he was also caring, kind and loving.

But then she'd known that from the first, hadn't she? From the morning when they'd first met, and he'd told her she was beautiful; the first time they'd made love, and he'd held her as she'd cried because he'd made her *feel* beautiful. From the genuine and enduring bond he'd formed with Aimee, to the way he'd risked his life with Charles to come to her rescue, he'd been selfless, and opened his heart to her without demanding anything in return except honesty. And now was the time to give it.

"He hit you? Charles hit you?" asked James of Pete, obviously impressed. "I didn't think anyone Charles hit would live to tell the tale. You must have a head like concrete."

"It has been said." Pete grinned.

Gemma half-laughed. "Hey, we're not talking about it."

"You might not be, but I am," said James.

But as soon as Gemma left them, James changed the conversation to Susie—Pete's former manager at his old winery of Whisper Creek which James now owned. Seems James had re-kindled an old relationship with Susie and had ended up hurting her, which he was cut up about.

James shook his head. "I messed up in California. Since we've returned, she refuses to speak to me."

"Seems pretty simple to me, James."

James raised an eyebrow. "Simple, you reckon?"

"Groveling, of course. All women like a good grovel."

James frowned and nodded. "I think I can grovel. I've never exactly done it before, but I could give it a try. Do you think that will be enough?"

Pete shrugged. "Not sure. Susie's pretty stubborn. Once she's made up her mind about something, she's difficult to shift."

James sighed. "Sure is. I've talked, I've tried to tell her what I feel, but she won't listen anymore."

"Ah, there's your answer."

"Where?"

"Stop talking and start *showing* her how much you feel."

For once James was at a loss for words. He was reduced to a perplexed grunt. Pete clapped him on the shoulder.

"Best of luck then, mate," said Pete and turned away, looking for Lizzi. The vast hall had filled up with friends, family and neighbors and he couldn't see her at first. Then a microphone crackled and he heard her clear her throat, just as Gemma lowered the volume on the music. Everyone turned with puzzled expressions to look at Lizzi.

What the hell was going on?

He shrugged and turned away. No doubt some words of thanks for Gemma and Callum.

The seeds of the plan had begun in an ambulance a week ago. And now, the seeds had sprouted, had grown into a full grown giant of a thing which scared the devil out of her. Because what was the thing she feared the most? Vulnerability. So what did she have to show to Pete? That she trusted herself with him, wholeheartedly. No more secrets. With this secret, there was nothing left for anyone else to know about her.

She glanced across at Pete. There was nothing for it but to *show* him she'd changed, that he'd changed her, and that she could be open, honest and... vulnerable. Then she caught Gemma's eye and nodded. Gemma was the only person who knew what was about to happen. Gemma grinned and turned down the music.

It was time for her big moment, and Lizzi stepped up onto the staircase and picked up the microphone that Gemma had left for her.

Lizzi cleared her throat. Unfortunately, she hadn't realized the microphone was already on, and the sound of her throat clearing came through the speakers. It certainly got people's attention, though. The noise fizzled out and all eyes were on her.

"Hi! Sorry to break into the evening, but I have something I'd like to say." She paused as she saw Aimee—her mouth open in surprise at seeing her mother commanding attention. "Aimee's been learning to swim recently, and her teacher told her it was 'sink or swim.'" She shrugged. "It's good advice. You don't know until you dive on in. And you have to risk the sinking to discover if you can swim. The options are simple. And that's why I'm here now—to make an announcement."

Max, who'd just arrived, looked up at her in amazement. Lizzi ignored him. She had to focus. Otherwise she'd never do it.

"Well," she modified. "It's more of a question than an announcement."

More people began to look toward her, intrigued.

"A question, Lizzi? What are you on about?" Max had pushed his way closer to her and stood, arms folded, a puzzled grin on his face as he watched his sister make a fool of herself.

"It's not a question for you, Max," she snapped, then remembered where she was and looked out to the crowd, searching for Pete. "It's a question that's usually asked in private. But I can't do that. Because you see, the person I'm asking it of, doesn't believe I trust him." She paused. "'Sink or swim'—and now, it's my turn."

A few people laughed, some of her friends mimed that she should switch off the microphone. But there was no way she was going to be dissuaded. Gemma stopped Callum from moving forward. If Lizzi was going to make a fool of herself then so be it. She had to get the message across to Pete in no uncertain terms, otherwise she could kiss a happy future goodbye. And this was the only way she could think of to do it.

Pete stood silently looking at her. She had no idea whether he'd heard or understood a single word she was saying. Desperate times called for desperate measures.

"Pete!" she yelled, pressing her mouth closer to the microphone. "Pete, this is a question for you."

Someone thumped Pete on the back and he frowned. She couldn't tell what feelings that frown might hide.

Whether he was still angry with her or not. The thought made her falter, and she cleared her throat once more.

"Pete! You said once that I should shout from the rooftops what I'm thinking, what I'm feeling. But I never have." She shrugged. "Too reserved... too *scared* of what people may think of me, I guess. Well, you're right. I'll do just about anything to stop myself being hurt, or humiliated, even building a big old wall around me to keep me safe. But you've shown me that while it might be safe inside that wall, it's lonely. Because it's a place where love can't enter." She took a deep breath. "So here I am, shouting from the rooftops. I love you, Pete Marshall, and I want to know if you want to marry me."

There was a collective pregnant pause while people let her words sink in. Then someone shouted. "So what do you say, Pete?"

Pete said something that she couldn't hear. But people around him laughed. She couldn't bear it. "What did you say?" she asked through the microphone.

He held his hands either side of his mouth. "I said, if you want to know if I'll marry you, you should go ahead and ask me."

She narrowed her eyes. How low did he want her to go? Very low, it seemed. She took another deep breath. "Will you marry me, Pete? I love you, and I want you to be by my side, sharing our lives forever. I trust you with my daughter. I trust you with my pride. I trust you with my heart and soul. Marry me. Please?"

"Ah." A collective sigh from the women was matched by laughter from the men.

Max shook his head and shouted over to Pete. "Put the girl out of her misery, Pete!"

Pete's face spread into a big grin and he said something which again she couldn't hear.

"Pete? What's your answer?" she said into the microphone.

The smile lines that she loved so much crinkled up around those blue eyes as he walked toward her. People parted as he approached. He stopped, cupped his mouth again and bellowed. "I will."

He walked up to her, took the microphone from her mouth to his and addressed the audience who were all watching now, laughing and grinning and talking. "And you're all invited to the wedding!"

With that, he tossed away the microphone, grabbed Lizzi's hand and walked her across to where Aimee, Gemma and Max and the others were gathered.

"Aimee, you okay here for a few hours, and we'll pick you up later?"

Aimee was laughing. Gemma came up behind and put her arm around her. "Great idea, isn't it Aimee? It'll give us time to work out what we're going to do for your mum's wedding. It'll take a lot of imagination to top this!" She shook her head in disbelief at Lizzi. "Well done, Lizzi. That was a corker."

Lizzi wiped the tears of embarrassment, confusion and happiness from her eyes and gave Gemma and Aimee a hug.

"That was the most cheesy thing I've ever seen, Lizzi," said Max shaking his head in disbelief. "But it worked!" He laughed as he gave her a big hug before turning to Pete. "And if you hadn't agreed to marry my big sister, you'd have had me to contend with."

"It was the only reason I agreed," laughed Pete. Lizzi elbowed him in the stomach. But Pete ignored the rebuke by sweeping her up in his arms. "Now Lizzi, it's time I took you away."

She pressed her blushing face against his chest as they walked out the open doors into the carpark. He set her on her feet when they reached the car, and opened the door for her.

"Where are we going?"

What he whispered into her ear made her melt inside.

"Can you say that again?" she asked faintly.

"I could go and grab that microphone and repeat what I've just said, if you like."

"No!"

He glanced at the people who'd gathered by the door to watch them leave. "I'm pretty sure they've all got a good idea where I'm taking you, anyway. Too late to blush, darling."

It *was* too late, and anyhow Lizzi didn't particularly feel like blushing. She felt like showing her man in every way she could how much she loved him, and how she wanted to give him. But this time, in private.

EPILOGUE

Two years later...

L izzi couldn't believe everyone had made it. The invitations had been sent out months earlier, hoping that the Mackenzie men, their families, and close friends, would be able to co-ordinate their schedules and be all in the same place together. It hadn't happened since Easter two years before. And that had been without Susie, James's wife, who was now very much part of the family.

And it had also been without Jonny—her six-month-old son who'd been named after her brother—who still showed no signs of sleeping through the night. She looked at him, snug in her arms, and he gave her a delicious smile which she made her forget her weariness. These past months may have been tiring, but they'd also been the best months of her life.

Aimee adored Jonny, and Lizzi could see a bond forming that she knew, from her experience with Max, would last a lifetime.

"Give Jonny to me," said Pete, putting his arm around

her waist and kissing her. "It's my turn and besides, you look tired. Go and sit, enjoy yourself. After all the hard work you've done organizing this, you should enjoy it, too."

"I *am* enjoying myself. Besides, it didn't feel like hard work. Especially not now we have a manager for the café."

But she knew it was an excuse of Pete's. Pete adored his son and insisted on having him every opportunity he could. So she handed Jonny to Pete who kissed him before holding him in his arms so he could look around at everyone—which he did. Jonny's eyes were wide as he took in the room full of children, and equally noisy adults.

"Well, we didn't have much choice about hiring a manager, did we? We need a good team to manage what the café's become."

Lizzi loved the way Pete always said "we" when he referred to the café. It showed her again and again, how wonderful it was to share her life with someone. And her café, which, as she looked around, she had to agree, had slowly grown into her vision—a beautiful space which showcased the best of local food, wines and art—and exceeded it, as far as profitability was concerned.

She kissed Pete on the cheek. "Thank you."

"For what?"

She shrugged. "Everything."

She wandered off leaving Pete to talk to James and Susie. She saw Cassandra outside on the lawn, trying to pull Lily out from the bottom of a pile of children. Lily emerged laughing and ran inside with the others, leaving Cassandra standing alone and exasperated. Seems if there was ever a group of children play-fighting, Lily was always at the center.

Lizzi beckoned Cassandra inside. "Come and have a glass of wine, you look as if you could do with one."

Cassandra smiled and shook her head as she walked inside. "That child of mine..."

"Will be absolutely fine. You'll see." She handed Cassandra a glass.

"Goodness, they're a noisy bunch, aren't they?" said Cassandra, looking around.

"That's because they're a happy bunch."

"Yes," said Cassandra, smiling as she watched Lily laughing at a joke Joe—Morgan and Rebecca's son—had made. "I guess they are."

"They are what?" asked Dallas as he slipped his arm around Cassandra's shoulders and kissed her. "Good-looking, sexy—"

Cassandra tutted and shook her head. "You always think we're talking about you."

He raised an eyebrow in mock rebuke. "I wasn't. I was talking about you!"

"Hey, everyone!" James called out. "Let's have a photo! It's the first time we have Lucia and Guy's twins Amaryllis and Xander with us, and"—he pulled a petite blonde toward him—"my lovely wife."

Susie rolled her eyes.

James ignored her. "Who, I'd like to announce is expecting our baby in June! A sister for Tom!"

If Cassandra thought they were noisy before, there was no word she could have described for the shouts and cheers and laughter that followed the announcement. James and Susie had been trying for a baby for a while, following the reversal of James's vasectomy. And now it had happened, sealing the day's happiness.

Lucia, with Amaryllis, and Guy, with Xander, came and congratulated Susie with big, heartfelt hugs. Lucia and Guy had been trying for a baby even longer than James and

Susie. It had taken years and many rounds of IVF treatment for Guy and Lucia to conceive, but they'd got their precious baby at last—two of them.

Only Cassandra's smile was a little subdued, shadowed by the sadness that was always with her. Her son, Danny, by her first husband, had been lost at sea years before but no body had ever been recovered. He would have been eleven years old now and she thought about him every day. Dallas was suddenly by her side, a supportive arm around her. Nothing was said, but everything was understood.

It took some organizing but eventually a tripod was found, the delay on the camera was figured out and, at last, they were all grouped together. The men—Dallas, Callum, James, Morgan, Guy and Pete—standing at the back with their arms proprietorially around their wives, as only these macho men could do.

In front of them, their children spilled out, not in orderly family groups, but all together, their closeness not bound by genetics alone.

Silence settled over the room as everyone smiled for the camera. Suddenly the sound of a phone's ringtone blasting out the theme song to Lily's favorite pop song, filled the air. Everyone burst into laughter and the flash went.

"Dallas!" said Cassandra. "Is that your phone?"

"Lily! You changed my ringtone again! Hey, sorry, everyone. Let's set up the shot again."

While James fiddled with the camera, Dallas picked up his phone and frowned as he looked at the caller ID. "Hey, won't be a moment. I need to take this."

The groans and words of teasing abuse followed Dallas outside. Lizzi saw Cassandra watch him pace the deck and suddenly stop, turn and look at her.

Lizzi felt the electricity in the air as Cassandra walked

out to meet him as if in a trance. Dallas's expression was unreadable.

"Dallas, tell me. What's happened?"

"It's Danny, Cassandra. He's been traced."

The world spun around, and Cassandra would have fallen if it hadn't been for Dallas holding her firm.

"What? What did you say?"

"Danny. He's okay. He's been suffering from memory loss, but it's returned. He remembers you. Your name. And more. And his adoptive parents traced you."

"No, no... I'm dreaming. It's not... true?" Tears ran down her face.

"It *is* true. Seems he was found washed up on the shore some distance from where the boat was last seen and has been taken care of by the same family all these years. He had a slight knock to the head recently, the only result of which was that his memory's been coming back in flashes. He remembers more each day. He's okay, Cassandra. He's well."

"How *can* it be him?"

"It is. They told me things that only he could know. About the last moments on the boat with your father. It *is* him."

"Hey, what's my Mum and Dad doing out there?" Lily asked Joe.

Joe swallowed another mouthful of the second meat pie that had found its way to his plate, and shrugged. "Looks like your mum's crying."

"Don't be stupid. You can't cry and laugh at the same time."

"You must be able to, because your dad's crying and laughing at the same time, too."

Lily frowned and folded her arms. "That's plain weird."

"Perhaps we should tell someone. I'll go and tell Dad; he always knows what to do."

"No, he won't, he's a man."

Joe pulled himself up to his full height which was considerably taller than Lily's. "Men know a lot."

"Not as much as women," said Lily, her green eyes flashing dangerously.

But Joe didn't rise to the bait. He looked Lily in the eyes, with the kind of cool that a matador must feel when faced with a rampaging bull. "Don't take on so, Lily. You know how it goes. Men know a lot of some stuff. Women know a lot of other stuff. And, when they get together, they know more."

"Hm," said Lily thoughtfully, the fire fading from her eyes. "I hadn't thought of it like that."

"Jeez," said Pete to Lizzi, as he caught the end of their conversation. "How did kids ever get so wise?"

"They'll grow out of it. They'll learn to be as stupid as adults before they grow wise again."

"And how does this magic transformation happen, Mrs. Marshall?"

"Through love, of course. How else?"

AFTERWORD

Thank you for reading *Summer at the Lakehouse Café,* the sixth and final book in **The Mackenzies** series. I hope you enjoyed it! The other books in the series are:

A Place Called Home (Guy and Lucia)
Secrets at Parata Bay (Dallas and Cassandra)
Escape to Shelter Springs (Callum and Gemma)
What you See in the Stars (Morgan and Rebecca)
Second Chance at Whisper Creek (James and Susie)
Summer at the Lakehouse Café (Pete and Lizzi)

Summer at the Lakehouse Café introduced Lizzi's family— the Connellys—who feature in my **Lantern Bay** series. An excerpt follows of *Yours to Give* which features Max, Lizzi's brother and his rollercoaster romance with Laura.

Happy reading!

Sophie

YOURS TO GIVE

BOOK 1 OF LANTERN BAY—MAX

YouTube sensation Laura McKinney has one goal—to live life to its fullest by accepting challenges from all around the world and filming them. She believes long-term relationships are for idiots, and marriage is ridiculous. Max Connelly reckons that makes her exactly his kind of woman.

But Max is pursuing his own dream, building his mountain resort into the place to be in the southern hemisphere. He knows what her publicity could do for his resort so he issues his own challenge—to get married. After all, it wouldn't mean anything to either of them. Would it?

Excerpt

Max Connelly narrowed his eyes against the bright sunlight and gave a long low whistle as a young woman tore by on a state-of-the-art mountain bike. She wore ripped jeans and a tiny top. Strands of long blonde hair escaped her safety helmet and flew behind her as she hurtled at breakneck speed down the steep grassy slope. Within seconds she'd reached the edge of the bluff and flew off, into the air.

Max held his breath like everyone else around him, waiting to see if she and her bike would part ways. Only the most experienced bikers ever attempted that jump. As she landed with a thud and a wobble, there was a collective outrush of amazement. But she didn't stop. Instead, she hurtled along the ridge, either side of which precipitous cliffs plunged.

Max gripped the balustrade of the terrace and cursed under his breath. Surely she wouldn't risk everything merely to get to the edge—a challenge reserved for only the most extreme sporting aficionados. At the last moment she twisted the bike around. Dust flew up around her as she jammed on her brakes and came to an abrupt halt at the very edge of the drop.

She gave a whoop of exultation and Max grinned—partly sharing her excitement and partly in relief. Her infectious laughter filled the small valley as she jumped off the bike and went to join her friends.

Without looking away from the woman, he placed his drink on the table and leaned over the balustrade of the Lodge's wide terrace, shaking his head in disbelief. "Did you see her? Man, she can move!"

"Max!" He looked around to find his sister, Lizzi, grinning at him. "Is that the owner's perk—checking out young women?"

"Who is she?" Max asked, ignoring her question. "An actress or model or something?"

"No idea. Whoever she is, she's popular. Looks like she's got quite a circle of admirers." Lizzi laughed. "Good luck with that one, bro!"

Max's eyes strayed back to the woman who'd unclipped her helmet and was shaking out her blonde hair. Like everyone else, he couldn't take his eyes off the girl.

The bright light seemed to emanate from her like an aura, but he knew it was more likely the effect of them being over five thousand feet up in the Southern Alps.

She was gorgeous. She was also either courageous or stupid—he didn't know which but he decided then and there he'd find out. And there was something else, another quality, which was totally disarming. She moved with an ease and unselfconsciousness, as if she had no clue how truly compelling she was. She tossed her helmet to someone and now stood, hands on slender hips, legs slightly apart. Not *girly* feminine, but definitely attractive. *Very* attractive.

"That's Laura McKinney," said Rachel, one of his other sisters who he'd managed to persuade to join him at his summer party at the mountain lodge. "She's the new YouTube sensation. She accepts dares and films them as she goes. She's quite something. Haven't you come across her? She's the darling of the media in the US. She's over here for a few weeks."

"In Queenstown? For a few weeks?" Max turned to Rachel. "How come I haven't heard of this?"

Rachel rolled her eyes. "An oversight of your staff, I'm sure."

"My staff managed to get *you* here. That's a near miracle." He frowned. "How did they manage to tear you away from Wellington, anyway?" It was as if a cloud descended on Rachel and she looked away. Max looked across at Lizzi to see if she was aware of a change in Rachel, but Lizzi was in a world of her own since she'd met Pete. He was glad but it didn't help him any. He made a mental note to find out what was bothering Rachel. But not now. Later. He looked back at the vision below him. "So how come they didn't tell me about the famous Laura McKinney? She could be good for business."

Rachel rested her folded arms on the railing and looked up at him. His first instinct was correct. Something *had* unsettled Rachel. He could see it in her eyes but before he could ask her what the matter was a cheer went up as waiters, carrying bottles of Champagne, approached Laura and the crowd which had gathered around her.

"Laura doesn't *do* planning. She arrives, she surprises, and then she's gone again. I doubt even Chelsey knew about Laura's intentions."

"Huh," grunted Max. "I pay her to know this kind of stuff."

"Why are you so annoyed?"

"Because that's the whole point of the summer party—to raise the Lodge's profile, to draw visitors to it—both summer and winter. That's why I have a PR team." He huffed an irritated sigh. "And, besides, I've made arrangements to leave for Australia in a couple of days."

"Ah, I get it," said Rachel. "Now you've seen Laura,

you'd prefer to hang out here, rather than enjoy Sydney's high life. Although, seriously, Max, I don't think Laura is your type."

Max frowned. "And what's my type?"

Rachel and Lizzi exchanged knowing glances. "You know. Super sophisticated, wealthy types. Jimmy Choo shoes, Birkin handbags, Ray-Ban sunglasses."

Max's frown deepened. "None of that means anything to me."

"No, but the type of women wearing them do."

"Give up, Rachel," said Lizzi. "He's a lost cause."

But Max was oblivious to their teasing and continued to watch the blonde below the terrace.

"You won't get anywhere there, Max, so I wouldn't even bother," said Rachel.

The idea of a woman turning him down was a new one to Max. "Why? Doesn't she like men?"

"Oh, she likes them all right. Likes them enough to insist that she'll never go out with anyone longer than a month. She's publicly stated that long-term relationships are for idiots and marriage is ridiculous."

"My kind of girl, then."

Rachel laughed and shook her head.

"See you later," said Max, descending the steps towards the blonde.

ALSO BY SOPHIE HAYDON

The Mackenzies

A Place Called Home

Secrets at Parata Bay

Escape to Shelter Springs

What you See in the Stars

Second Chance at Whisper Creek

Summer at the Lakehouse Café

Lantern Bay

Yours to Give

Yours to Treasure

Yours to Cherish

Yours to Keep

Yours Forever

Yours to Love

ABOUT THE AUTHOR

Hello!

My name is Sophie Haydon and I write romances with stories which make you turn the pages, and characters who feel real.

I'm an avid people watcher, hopeless romantic and dreamer who spends far too much time gazing out the window, imagining scenes where people struggle with life and emotions but always end up happily. Because, yes, I'm also an eternal optimist!

I currently have two connected series — Mackenzies and Lantern Bay — which feature the Mackenzie and Connelly families. At the moment, I'm writing the fifth Lantern Bay book, but am already planning future series.

All the books I've written so far are set in New Zealand, where I live. But I was born on the north Norfolk coast of England and am planning a series set in the small seaside town in which I grew up. And then there's my Nantucket trilogy which I began planning years ago, but have yet to find time to write.

So, wherever you are in the world, welcome to my little corner, where I sit with my two cocker spaniels snoring gently beside me, creating worlds where people struggle with life and emotions but are always rewarded with love and happiness in the end. Because that's non negotiable!

I hope you enjoy my books.

Sophie

x